About the author

John T Leonard continues to write under a pseudonym. The reason for this is because he is a serving British Police Officer. He is conscious that his ongoing projects may taint his involvement in any current or future investigations. It does remain his ambition to one day become a full-time writer and to potentially re-release his work under his real name.

He is a divorced father of two young children. He currently lives in the south of England.

Leonard continues to suffer with his mental health, and during the writing of this project he succumbed to his affliction and relented to take his first absence due to it. He remains outspoken about mental health issues affecting Emergency Service workers and is an advocate for better working conditions for them.

A LIFE'S WORK

Valentijner You
Thanks for
Support - keep
your eyes open
to future releases

2019

Also by John T Leonard

Settling the Score

Primus

John T Leonard

A LIFE'S WORK

Vanguard Press

A CIP catalogue record for this title is
available from the British Library.

ISBN 978 1 784655 06 8

*Vanguard Press is an imprint of
Pegasus Elliot MacKenzie Publishers Ltd.*
www.pegasuspublishers.com

First Published in 2018

**Vanguard Press
Sheraton House Castle Park
Cambridge England**

Printed & Bound in Great Britain

For Nathaniel and Evangeline

Chapter One
Oliver, aged 5

"Ladies and Gentlemen of the jury, this trial has been harrowing for us all. During the time we have spent in this courtroom we have heard how the defendant, Marc Sullivan, attacked his victim, beating her senseless, before raping her and then leaving her to die from her injuries. All this time her five-year-old son was strapped into his seat in the car only yards from where his mother's body was eventually found. Sullivan then made attempts to steal her car, which only achieved one thing, and that was for him to come face-to-face with a terrified child, whose mother he had just taken from him."

The barrister for the prosecution then felt compelled to turn his back on the jury and face Sullivan who was sitting in the dock, flanked by two court officers. He then continued.

"The five-year-old boy was untouched during the brutal and callous attack which claimed his mother's life, but regardless of the lack of any physical involvement, he still remains the second victim of this heinous atrocity. He remains in a catatonic state from witnessing this ordeal. *His* ordeal of hearing his mother attacked and brutalised mere yards from him, hearing her screams subdued and silenced as she is rendered unconscious and eventually succumbing to her injuries."

He turned again to face the jury and paced the length of their bench.

"He was only five years old, almost six now to be more precise. What possible recollection could he have of such awful events? But look at it through his eyes, his parents are the light of his life, their laughter brings him joy, and their tears bring him sorrow. So, what must his mother's screams of terror bring him? And more so, what about when they're silenced forever. When a crazed attacker leaves him helpless and alone in the middle of nowhere, with no one to call to for help."

He paused to allow the gravity of his continued account to sink into the parents amongst the jurors, if no one else.

"Imagine that it's you that's left alone, you're helpless and unable to fend for yourself. You cry out, calling out towards the lifeless body of your mother left strewn, beaten and naked just yards beyond where you can see outside of the car that now holds you prisoner. Then by sheer chance you're able to survive long enough, long enough to enable you to be found and rescued. But your ordeal is far from over. In fact, it's only just beginning. It's been over six months since that awful night, and this once vivacious and loquacious child hasn't uttered a sound in anything other than pain and misery. He remains incapable of showing any joy or happiness. So please, Ladies and Gentlemen, when you retire to consider your verdict, I want you to remember that there are two victims in this case, not just Mary Bennett. I want you to also keep her son Oliver firmly in your minds when you deliberate to reach a verdict. The Crown rests, and I thank you."

The barrister for the prosecution stood motionless for a moment, before turning and returning to his seat at his bench. He had to walk past the defence's barrister to retake his seat. They exchanged the briefest of acknowledgements. The defence had given their closing argument first, but it would be the prosecution's heart-rending account that would stand fast in their minds as they retire. The prosecution's barrister had seen what he had hoped he would during his speech; a look of disdain on the faces of the jury. They too were appalled by the evidence, and the testimonies they had heard throughout the two weeks of the trial that had led to this point. The end was in sight for them all.

"All rise," the court usher cried.

Everyone stood as directed. The judge was the first to leave the Court Room for his chambers, followed immediately by the members of the Jury through a different door.

The defence team then turned to see the defendant, Marc Sullivan escorted from the dock back down to the cells below the Courts by the court officers who had stood dutifully beside him throughout the session.

oOo

The deliberation of juries to reach their verdict has been known to take days, even weeks. Sometimes, they would request Court transcripts to be read out or exhibits shown to them in their chambers to clarify testimonies or evidence presented. In a trial of this length this wasn't unheard of, as the first witness could have taken the stand very early on in the trial and the jury's recollection could be weak, as weeks could have passed.

The physical evidence can also be revisited as required. Photos and videos can be shown and replayed as and when needed, sometimes several times.

However, none of that was needed today. After only twenty-three minutes of deliberation by the jury the Court was called back in.

This appeared to shock and unnerve the prosecution in equal measure. They felt they had a strong case against Sullivan, but even so, they expected a much longer deliberation. They had prepared for a longer recess, as was evident when the barrister was caught in the middle of his lunch when they were called back in.

After the Court session resumed, the judge addressed the jury. "Have you reached a verdict to which you all agree?" he asked.

The nominated spokesperson, or head juror, stood and responded accordingly, "Yes, we have, Your Honour."

The usher approached the head juror and took a folded piece of paper that was being presented by her. The usher then walked over to where the judge sat and handed him the piece of paper. The judge unfolded it, read what was on it, before handing it back to the usher, who in turn handed it back to the head juror.

"In the matter of The Crown versus Sullivan what say you?" the judge asked of the jury.

The head juror cleared her throat before responding. "In the matter of The Crown versus Sullivan on the charges of the rape and murder of Mary Bennett, we the jury find the defendant," there was a slight pause for nothing more than to catch a breath, "guilty."

Although the verdict was expected by most, there was still a hush that had fallen over the Court.

The judge then thanked the members of the jury for their service. He then scheduled a sentencing hearing where Sullivan would once again appear before the Court.

The gavel came down, and the Court was dismissed.

Chapter Two
Oliver, aged 13

"Hello," came the greeting as the phone was answered.

"Hello, sir," came the reply, "is this Mr Bennett?"

"Yes, it is, who's this?"

"Sir, I am PC Harvey from Longbranch Police Station, are you the father of an Oliver Bennett?" the officer asked.

"Yes, I am, what's he done now?"

"Now? He's been in trouble before...? Never mind," the officer retracted his own question having considered the irrelevancy of it, "are you able to come down to the police station? We have arrested Oliver and need you to act as an appropriate adult so he can be interviewed."

"What's he s'posed to have done?" asked Mr Bennett.

"I can't go into detail about this over the phone. Are you able to come down to the police station, sir? I'll be able to explain everything to you when you get here."

"I guess I don't have any choice in the matter, now do I?" Mr Bennett said rhetorically. "When do you need me there?"

"As soon as possible really, sir. Are you going to want a solicitor? The only reason I ask now is if that is the case then I can get one sorted to speed things up a bit," the officer said.

"Have you got him in a cell?

"Yes, sir, we do."

"Then there's no real rush then is there, hopefully this'll teach him a lesson in itself." Mr Bennett lowered the phone to check his watch. It said 4:43 p.m. He lifted the phone to his face again. "I can be there for about five thirty. I'll decide about the solicitor when I get there, if that's ok?"

As he ended the call and hung up by replacing the handset in its cradle, a grimace of frustration came over his face.

"I'll fucking kill him," he said as he shook his head disapprovingly. He had already convicted and sentenced his son and only child, Oliver, before even knowing under what circumstances he had been arrested.

Mr Bennett looked at his watch again and realised he had been overly optimistic in his estimation of when he would arrive at Longbranch Police Station. He only lived about five miles away, but given the time of day, he would now have to contend with the evening rush hour. On top of which, he had absolutely no intention of rushing in order to spare his son from spending an extra hour or two in a police cell. He reaffirmed his earlier sentiment to himself. It *would* do him some good to spend some time in a police cell.

He realised it was already lucky for Oliver that he was even at home. He'd had a meeting with a prospective client locally which had finished ahead of time. Had this not been the case, either he would have had to come home to a message, or the police may have been able to reach him on his mobile, had Oliver been able to provide them with his number.

Mr Bennett went back to the table in the dining room which he was using as a makeshift office. He hovered over his laptop, propping himself up with one arm resting on the table. He then used a remote mouse to drag the cursor over to the corner of the screen to close down the spreadsheet he had opened. But before he did, he realised it wasn't quite ready to be shut down. If he were to return to this screen as it was, it may not be immediately apparent where he had last left it.

Despite his earlier sentiment, Mr Bennett now had no choice but to retake his seat at the table in order to add a few more entries to the spreadsheet before being able to shut it down. He was now confident that he would know exactly where to pick it up from when he would eventually return to it. After closing down the laptop and finishing what was left of his coffee, which was in the mug next to his makeshift work area, he stood up and walked out of the dining room and into the hallway.

Having not long been home from the customer appointment, he still had his shoes on. So, all that was needed was to grab his coat from the hall closet.

Once he had his coat on, he went back to the kitchen and reclaimed his keys and wallet from the side. He was now as ready as he'd ever be.

This wasn't the first time he had been in this situation. But, like every time that had come before, he was ever hopeful it would be the last. He wasn't intending to come across to the police officer on the phone as being unduly harsh on Oliver, or the situation. He wasn't even angry with his son, despite not even knowing the situation or the reason he had been arrested. He acted out of frustration as opposed to anger. He just knew something needed to change. Neither he nor Oliver could go on like this.

oOo

During the drive to the police station, Mr Bennett reminisced about the previous occasions that the police had been involved in his and Oliver's lives.

He thought back to the last time that he had to attend a police station to act as an appropriate adult for Oliver, to sit in on his son's recorded interview under caution in order to ensure that his son was not bullied during the process, or coerced into admitting to anything.

As an appropriate adult he was required to act on behalf of the subject, Oliver, as he was under the age of eighteen years, or older if deemed to be vulnerable by means of infirmity or mental health.

The previous occasion was only a few months earlier, during the school holidays. Oliver had been detained, but not arrested, after being found as one of a group of boys who matched the description of children who were seen to be practicing *free-running,* or *Parkour,* across the roofs of a school building.

Parkour is a training discipline developed in France which uses movements that are developed from military obstacle course training. Practitioners are known as *traceurs,* and their aim is to get from one point to another in any complex environment, without assistive equipment and in the fastest and most efficient way possible. Parkour includes running, climbing, swinging, vaulting, jumping, rolling, and movements on all fours, and other movements as deemed most suitable for the situation.

Only because there was no damage caused, and because Oliver was polite and cooperative when the police approached him, added to which he made no attempt to run off like the others did, he was merely brought home and spoken to by officers in front of his father. However, neither his father nor the police were happy with the fact that Oliver refused to divulge the names of those also involved when he was asked to do so.

This protection, however, wasn't long-lived. For when school resumed the police went in and viewed the CCTV from the incident. Then with the assistance of staff, they were able to identify another child from the original group, and he wasn't as noble as Oliver had been. He was more than enthusiastic when it came to giving up his friends in order to save his own neck. As a result, when the dust settled on the parkour incident, those identified went looking for some payback from the friend who had given them up, and he, in turn, tried to implicate Oliver. But nothing ever ended up coming back to Oliver.

Oliver was very capable of learning lessons as his father was well aware. Spending time on his own in a police cell was intended to be for his own good.

Mr Bennett had always done the best he could, both for himself and Oliver since the trial. Oliver had always been his number one priority, sometimes much to his own detriment.

In the eight years since the tragic events that had decimated his family, Paul Bennett had tried to find love again. But his loyalty was always to his son. The closest he had come to finding a companion ended as a result of Oliver's unruly behaviour. His partner didn't understand the trauma that Oliver had been through. She was adamant that it was solely a case of *boys needing discipline.* This didn't sit well with Paul, and as a result drove a wedge between them and the rest was inevitable.

That relationship ended a couple of years ago, and since then he appeared to prefer the company of a glass or two of Scotch in the evening instead of female company.

oOo

As he pulled into one of the visitors parking bays at Longbranch Police Station he looked at the clock on the dashboard display. It read 17.52, he checked his watch thinking the time was inaccurate, but instead it only served to reaffirm it.

Mr Bennett entered the front office of the police station. It was set out like a doctor's waiting room, a single desk behind a protective glass partition with microphones and speakers, and a couple of rows of chairs along the walls. There were three people sat there, it was impossible to tell if they had already been seen or were still waiting to speak to the office clerk.

Mr Bennett was about to take a seat and wait his turn when he saw a telephone mounted on the wall next to doors which were marked *interview rooms*.

The instructions on the phone encouraged those who had an extension number, or the name of a specific officer to pick up the phone and either dial the extension or dial 0 and to ask for that officer.

Mr Bennett picked up the receiver, he dialled 0 and when the call was answered he asked for PC Harvey. After a brief conversation, he replaced the receiver and took a seat.

After a minute or so, a uniformed police officer entered the front office via an internal door. "Mr Bennett," he called out, not knowing who in the room he was actually addressing.

"Yes," Paul Bennett replied, as he rose to his feet. The officer approached him where he now stood, he extended a hand, which Mr Bennett shook.

After the introductions, PC Harvey led Mr Bennett back out of the Front Office, through the door he had originally entered, and around the side of the police station towards the secured entrance to the custody suite.

The officer then began to explain to Mr Bennett his role and responsibilities in acting as Oliver's appropriate adult.

"Your key role and responsibility is to support and advise Oliver, both before and during the actual interview, you're there to observe whether the police are acting appropriately, and to assist with any communication issues between Oliver and the police. And, to ensure that Oliver understands his rights, you also have a role in protecting those rights."

By the time this was explained and understood, PC Harvey had led Mr Bennett into the custody suite and to a consultation room. He held open the door and gestured to Mr Bennett to take a seat.

"I'll have Oliver brought in to you, okay, do you want a coffee or something?" PC Harvey said.

"Please, any chance you can Irish it up a bit?" he said in a failed attempt at humour, that evidently missed its mark with PC Harvey.

The consultation room itself was sparse in its furnishings, it had a small table to one side which was bolted to the floor, and on both sides of the table were bolted down benches, each just wide enough for two people to sit on. Mr Bennett sat down on the far bench so he had a view of the door.

After a couple of minutes, Oliver was brought into the consultation room by PC Harvey. Mr Bennett stood as he saw his son. They both took the necessary couple of steps towards each other so they could hug. This was indication enough to PC Harvey that Oliver was safe to be left alone with his father. He had to assess the dynamic between them in order to determine that his father was indeed appropriate for the role he had been brought in for. PC Harvey left the room, allowing the door to close behind him.

Oliver sat down across from his father. For the briefest of moments, they sat in silence before his father felt compelled to banish it. He said in the calmest of voices, "So, c'mon then tell me why we're here this time?"

"Dad, I didn't do anything. Honest! I was just messing about with a dead fox, I was just poking at it, it was dead when I got there."

"And...?" his father said trying to prompt some elaboration, feeling there had to be more to it than that. He felt surely there had to be more to it than what Oliver had just volunteered.

"That's it! Its belly had burst open, and I was just having a poke around inside. I'm walking away when the *Po* rock up and stop me. They go on about some cat killer and then they nick me."

"The *Po*?"

"The *Po*, y'know, *Po-Po*, the police," Oliver replied matter-of-factly, bordering insolent.

Before his father could reply, there was a knock at the door. Mr Bennett could see through the glass that it was PC Harvey. He didn't need to be let in, but it was a courtesy under legislation that a conversation between the suspect and their advisor had to be a privileged conversation. PC Harvey was holding a coffee with one hand and some papers with the other. Once he received an acknowledgement from Mr Bennett, he entered the room.

"I need both of you to come up to the desk so we can go through Oliver's rights and entitlements."

First his father, and then Oliver stood and walked towards the door.

Although Oliver had already been booked in when he first arrived at custody following his arrest, he had to be booked in again with his father present. The booking-in process covered the details of the arrest, the circumstances of the arrest, and why the arrest was necessary. The former was no longer of news to Mr Bennett, however, the actual reason for Oliver's arrest still eluded him. The arrest necessity at this stage was just described as being *to allow a prompt and effective investigation.*

The booking-in process also covered Oliver's right to have a solicitor present during the interview, or at least speak to one prior to being interviewed. Mr Bennett chose to decline both options. This prompted an approving smile on the face of PC Harvey as he could now interview Oliver without any further delay. Had a solicitor been required then that could've led to a delay of up to a couple of hours.

After the booking-in was completed, PC Harvey asked if Mr Bennett was ready to go to interview, to which he replied that he was.

During the interview, PC Harvey began by again explaining why Oliver had been arrested. This reiterated the circumstances as read out during the booking-in process. Oliver listened intently as PC Harvey explained that over the previous few months a number of cats had been found dismembered and mutilated in a widening area around Oliver's school. He further explained how most of the mutilations appeared to have taken place at night, only for the gruesome discovery to be found the following morning.

PC Harvey admitted that they didn't have anything to currently identify an offender. A description had yet to be provided, as so far there had been no witnesses. He did state that as yet unidentified human blood had been found near to the scene of the most recent incident. But this was considered as circumstantial evidence.

PC Harvey then stated that a member of the public had seen Oliver interfering with an animal carcass and believed it may connect to the mutilations.

"Then why not just bring him home, for us to have this little chat there?" Mr Bennett enquired.

"Because of the blood sample found at the most recent scene, we need to ask Oliver to provide a specimen of blood for comparison, and that can only be done when he's in custody." PC Harvey paused. "Do you agree for us to take some of Oliver's blood?"

"Okay, let me get this straight, you've arrested my thirteen-year-old son because he was seen poking a dead fox, and now you want him to give you a blood sample because you think he might be responsible for killing cats. Is that about the size of it?"

Mr Bennett looked over at his son. The look he got in response from his son told him everything he needed to know. Mr Bennett then addressed PC Harvey again. "Please tell me you have something more to link my son to these killings…"

"No, Mr Bennett, that's it, we just want to be able to rule your son out from the blood found at the scene," PC Harvey replied.

"And even if it was a match to the blood, what would it prove? That at some point my son was in the street and dripped blood near to where a dead cat was found?" He paused long enough to expect a response from PC Harvey. When none came, he continued.

"My answer is *no!* I am *not* going to subject my son to that just so you can look like you're making a breakthrough until this is no longer front-page news."

This concluded the interview. PC Harvey then took Oliver and his father back to the same consultation room as before whilst he reviewed the investigation and had a decision made over Oliver's detention.

oOo

Within an hour Oliver found himself being driven home in his dad's car. They had gone via a drive-through burger restaurant in order to give him a treat to make up for the unpleasantness of the day.

Oliver had been released *under investigation*. This meant that he was still linked to the investigation as a *possible* suspect, so that he could be called upon in the future should things progress in any given direction. He was not given any restrictions such as a curfew or having to report to a police station periodically. Both he and his father were advised that should Oliver be recalled with regards to the investigation and refuse to comply in any way, he could find himself subject to further arrest.

Oliver's father had absolutely no doubt in his mind that his son had nothing to do with these incidents. Oliver loved animals, and any alleged behaviour to the contrary would be abhorrent to him.

They had a pet cat at home until its death of old age a couple of years earlier. It had been discussed, and ruled out against getting another pet, as it would prevent them both from being able to take off at a moment's notice on a break or holiday should the desire take them. Not that had *ever* happened in the time since the creature's demise.

Later that evening, as Oliver's father was about to settle down for bed, he walked past his son's closed bedroom door. He felt a draught coming out from under the door which chilled his bare ankles. This was unusual. He stopped at the door and listened. He could hear no noises coming from within Oliver's bedroom. He knocked at the door and waited. No response. He took hold of the handle and pressed it downwards, the latch released and the door fell inwards.

The room was in darkness, the TV was on, it was on mute or the volume had been turned all the way down, there was light but no sound. Opposite the door the curtains were closed, they were billowing in and out over an open window.

Mr Bennett hurried across the room to part the curtains. He looked out of the open window across the back garden. Oliver was nowhere to be seen.

Given the events of the day, and knowing his son as he did, he knew exactly what Oliver was up to, and where he was likely to find him. He also knew that the police did not need to be involved in locating him.

Mr Bennett reclosed the curtains. He was very meticulous to leave Oliver's room exactly as he had found it.

He then made adjustments to suggest that he himself had gone to bed before leaving the house by the front door. He turned on his bedside lamp and closed his door. From the hallway, a warm glow emanated from under his bedroom door, obvious for all to see.

Knowing he also had to leave the car on the driveway to avoid alerting Oliver should he return before his father, Mr Bennett began to walk in the direction of Oliver's school, in the direction that the recently reported incidents for which he had been arrested had taken place. He knew where to find his son, and why he had sneaked out at that time of night.

Chapter Three
Oliver, aged 9

"Not you again, Bennett, come on in, what is it this time?" The headmaster tried to look authoritative as he ushered Oliver into his office. He stood with his back to the open door, he towered over the diminutive child as he walked past him.

Oliver had been sent to the headmaster's office clutching a piece of paper; this was the report from his teacher as to why he had been sent to see the headmaster. He placed it between his teeth as he did his best to straighten his uniform, it was untucked and ruffled and torn.

The headmaster, Mr Shean, then allowed the door to close and circled around the back of his large desk to stand across from Oliver. He took a seat on the far side. He encouraged Oliver to also sit. He then leant over the desk to take the note from Oliver and began to read it.

Oliver maintained his dignity throughout as he handed over the piece of paper and watched as Mr Shean read it. His gaze never averted from a respectful, but not defiant look directly towards his headmaster.

Oliver could see Mr Shean's eyes scanning from left to right, from left to right. He smiled momentarily, realising he was only a short step from having his lips silently mouth the words as he read them. He did, however, stifle the smile as soon as it had emerged as he didn't want the headmaster to consider it an act of insolence. He knew what he had done was wrong, but with good reason.

"So," Mr Shean broke the silence, "you've been fighting *again*. Start from the beginning, tell me what happened."

"Well, sir…"

oOo

"I had come to school and left my bike at the rack behind the science block. It's a bit beat up, my bike, I mean it's a decent enough bike an' all, but it does look a bit tatty now.

"Anyway, I went to class and right from first register Callum Baxter is riding me. He's taking the mickey out of my bike. He's saying it's a piece of crap and stuff like that. Ms Beaumont will be able to tell you that, she told him to knock it off.

"First period, me and him are in different groups, right, so nothing's said. Then at morning break, him and a couple of his lot start at me again. This time, sir, they start pushing me. I didn't do anything back to them.

"Then at lunchtime, I was a bit upset, so I went where I know we're not supposed to go during the day. I went round to the bike rack. I only went there to be on my own, but I see Keiron and his lot there.

"I didn't want to do anything, but they saw me before I could get outta there. I could see they were near my bike, and he started pulling at it in the rack.

"I told him to stop, but he kept doing it.

"I told him again, he then says 'What are you gonna do, get your mommy and daddy to come to the school or something?'

"He then said, 'Oh, wait, you don't have a mommy, do ya!'

"He then started laughing. That's when I hit him.

28

"When I hit him the others just ran.

"I just kept hitting him. He fell down, I kept hitting him.

"He screamed for me to stop, I just kept hitting him.

"Then he stopped screaming, I stopped too."

oOo

Mr Shean paused before saying anything. Across the desk from him was nine-year-old Oliver Bennett in tears, his face buried in his hands. His shoulders shaking uncontrollably. His sobs most likely being heard in the next office and possibly the corridor.

Mr Shean was fully aware of Oliver's past. But he was just a middle school headmaster. He schooled normal children aged eight to twelve years, never had he had one with such tragedy behind them. As a result, he had no specific training to deal with him as such.

Mr Shean waited until what he felt was an opportune time to say something. He knew he had to say something, but he wasn't sure what. Oliver's father had been called, so any questioning of Oliver's account should wait, but he had to address the sobbing child in front of him.

"How do you feel about what happened?" Mr Shean eventually asked.

Oliver raised his face from his hands. Mr Shean could see the light from the window behind him glisten off the tears forming a stream down Oliver's cheeks.

Oliver appeared unable to verbalise a response. Upon making eye contact he just shook his head, before sobbing again, before feeling the need to cover his face with his hands once more.

Mr Shean was a father himself, to a teenage son, and a daughter of about Oliver's age. He felt the pain of seeing a child in such distress, and feeling so helpless to offer comfort and safety.

As much as he wanted to walk around his desk and give physical reassurance to this child, he knew he couldn't.

Decorum dictated that he must remain professional and impartial. He had only received one account of the incident. He had yet to speak to Callum or any of his friends. He couldn't be seen to take sides, no matter how painful that was for him.

It came with a sense of relief when there came a knock at his office door.

"Come." Mr Shean paused and coughed to clear his throat, "COME IN," he now said with renewed authority.

The door opened and the school secretary entered; she then held the door open for Oliver's father, Mr Bennett, to enter.

Oliver turned to face his father. His father looked down at him. No anger or defiance existed between them, only compassion and regret.

Mr Bennett stood beside his son to show his support, he extended a hand to Mr Shean.

"Paul Bennett," he said as Mr Shean shook his hand.

"Giles Shean," came the reply, "please take a seat."

Mr Shean then asked to excuse himself so that he could converse with other staff on the matter, as well as having the opportunity to speak to Callum who was currently in the medical room. His parents had also been requested to attend, but he did not know if either of them had as yet arrived.

Once Oliver and his father had the room to themselves, his father pirouetted on one foot to stand with his back to the desk and leant back and propped himself against it. He began tapping his fingers against the top.

With the mixed emotion of the situation that had earlier faced the headmaster, Paul Bennett ensured he was composed before saying anything. This was to ensure he was able to convey himself with compassion for his upset son, yet maintaining an air of authority until he had a full understanding of the situation.

"We've got a few minutes until he comes back, why don't you tell me what happened."

Oliver sniffled a couple of times, he made attempts to wipe his face. On seeing this, his father glanced around the office. He saw a box of tissues on the desk, just out of reach. He stood up, moved around the desk, and plucked one tissue, then another from the box before moving to within range of Oliver, and handed them to him. He then returned to his original position, so not to be felt as imposing to Oliver.

After a moment or two of face wiping came the inevitable nose blow, before muffled words came from behind the protection afforded by the tissue.

"He was teasing me about Mum," Oliver said.

"Aaaaahhhhhhhhh," replied his father trying not to sound in any way judgmental, now realising what he was dealing with. In an instant, everything became clear. Until now, the mere mention of his mother in any context had resulted in an extreme emotional reaction from Oliver, usually an accentuation of what had immediately preceded it. But what had preceded it? In this situation, he still needed to find out.

"Walk me through it, Ollie, tell me what happened, take your time, there's no rush." He paused. "Y'know, I'd rather hear it from you than your headmaster when he comes back in."

Oliver was silent as he repeated the cleansing process before reciting the account as he had earlier given the headmaster.

After his account was given, there was a moment of silence as Paul Bennett absorbed the last of what he had just heard.

"What made you stop hitting him?" his father asked.

"When he stopped screaming for me to stop, I knew he'd had enough," Oliver replied.

This remark had hard-hitting ramifications for his father. Paul Bennett was in Court for most of Marc Sullivan's trial. He had witnessed the testimony given by the man who had ended his wife's life and nearly cost his son *his* life.

Under cross-examination by the prosecution, the defendant had stated under oath to the Court that the only reason he had stopped beating the victim, Bennett's wife, was when she fell silent and had stopped thrashing beneath him. He had said 'It was no longer a challenge when she stopped fighting back.' He then said, 'There's no sport in that.'

This experience nearly destroyed him, taking Bennett to the brink of desperation, it led him to drink excessively, which cost him at least one job. But it had to be done, it was for him, like so many before him, and no doubt since, a coping mechanism. Known to be counter-productive and unhealthy, but necessary in the circumstances.

This would be the only opportunity he would have to look directly at the face of the man who had destroyed his family. Like the prosecution had summated, there was not only one victim of the charge Sullivan was on trial for, the victims of such a crime are far-reaching. As a result, both he and Oliver continued to suffer and endure their pain both collectively and as individuals.

There was another silence, nothing more needed to be said between Oliver and his father, each of them knew all they needed to.

They were enjoying the silence, perhaps too much, when it was broken as the door opened, and Mr Shean re-entered his office.

Paul Bennett jumped like a child caught red-handed in the act, he was still perched on the corner of the headmaster's desk. He jumped to his feet, standing almost to attention.

He caught a slight smile on the face of Mr Shean having noticed his action. Shean then saw Bennett's reaction which saw him in turn smiling.

Mr Shean went back around his desk and sat down. He gestured towards a chair in a corner for Mr Bennett to use. It had been there all along, but Mr Bennett hadn't noticed it.

He picked it up from where it was and placed it a short distance and at a favourable angle to where Oliver sat, and took a seat.

When Mr Shean was sure everyone was receptive he began to explain the situation to them.

"Mr Bennett, Oliver," he began, "despite the severity and complexities of this situation, one factor above all else is abundantly clear, and has a huge bearing on the situation, and any outcome."

Mr Shean paused there as if expecting some reaction from the Bennetts; if he was waiting for one, he was to be disappointed. Both sat calm and united.

He continued, "The one factor is your age, Oliver, you're nine years old, granted not far off your tenth birthday, but you *are* nine years old, which means under the eyes of the Law you are not criminally responsible for your actions. As a result, we do not need to go into the intricacies of the situation as far as apportioning blame et cetera."

There was still nothing to be seen in the way of any reaction from the Bennetts.

"The other boy involved has admitted provoking you, but that does not exclude you from your responsibilities in this matter. And having spoken to his mother, she does not feel the need to take this matter beyond this office. She has already left the school with her son, she's taking him to have him checked over at the hospital…"

This remark did have a physical reaction from Oliver. His eyes opened wide in shock. The mere mention of the word hospital dropped the gravity of the situation on him all in one go. His actions had caused someone to have to be taken to hospital.

Although he didn't show it, Mr Shean was pleased to see this reaction, it went some way to demonstrating remorse from him. Despite the contributing factors, remorse suggested an understanding and an empathy for what had taken place.

"Oliver, what I am going to suggest is that your father takes you home now and, let me see, today is Wednesday, that you come back to school fresh on Monday; that will give you time to reflect on what has happened today, give you time to think about how you can avoid things like this in the future. How does that sound to you?"

Oliver nodded his agreement. He didn't see this as a punishment. He saw that his headmaster had a clear understanding of what he was going through.

"Mr Bennett, I'm having the secretary dig out contact details for some counsellors for you, I would suggest at the very least making contact with them to see for yourself if you feel they could be of any help to you and Oliver."

"Thank you," came the reply, "I'll do just that, you have my word."

"I think, unless you have any questions for me, we're done here…?" Mr Shean said rising to his feet.

Mr Bennett shook his head. "I don't think so," he said as he too stood up.

"Well, should you have any questions, then please do get in touch," Mr Shean said as he walked around his desk towards the office door.

"C'mon, Ollie," his father said as he put a hand on his son's shoulder as he was still sat down, "let's get you home, eh?"

Oliver stood, and as he turned he could see Mr Shean had already opened the door and was in the process of shaking hands with his father again.

Beyond the door was the entrance lobby of the school. Normally children were not allowed to use this as an exit, but the area was busy with children. Oliver felt they must be there to see him marched out.

Oliver stepped forward, he felt Mr Shean's hand on his shoulder as he approached the doorway. "I'll see you on Monday." Oliver offered no reply.

The conversation between his father and his headmaster became muffled and consumed by the whispers coming from the lobby.

"There he is," said one.

"That's him," said another.

Oliver looked at the many faces staring at him. He froze.

It was then he felt the reassurance of his father's hand on his shoulder.

"Let's get you home," he said as he led Oliver out of the front door of the school.

Chapter Four
Oliver, aged 9

"Good morning, Oliver, my name is Yvonne. Thank you for coming in to see me today. I'm hoping these sessions are something you feel you'll be able to benefit from. We're hopefully going to be getting to know a lot about each other over the coming weeks and months. But to start with, why don't you tell me a little bit about yourself, what you like doing, what you don't like to do, why you think you're here, and how you feel being here could benefit you."

There was a long silence as Yvonne Martin, child therapist and psychologist looked across at Oliver slumped in the chair opposite her.

They were sat in the conservatory of her home, surrounded by plants. They were seated on wicker chairs, with a wicker and glass coffee table between them. The conservatory had blinds, which were closed to shield them both from the low sun in the morning sky.

After Oliver had finished exploring the room with his gaze, he finally showed a response to the questions he had been asked.

"Why am I here?" he said rhetorically in a soft voice.

"Why – am – I – here?" he said again slower than before, as if for his own understanding.

"I know why *I'm* here!" he said defiantly. "Why do *you* think I'm here?" he asked of Yvonne.

"Okay, Oliver, have it your way, I think you're here because you're having trouble coming to terms with what has happened around you. I think you're here because, somehow, you're taking responsibility for what has happened, despite being only five years old at the time, you feel you should've acted in some way to prevent those awful things from having actually taken place. I feel you are tormented by your recollections of that night, and your rage is in some way intended to vindicate yourself of any guilt you may be feeling. Any of this sounding familiar?"

There was absolutely no response from Oliver whose gaze was now fixated on a small gap in the blinds, searching for a world beyond the conservatory.

Oliver knew he had to attend these sessions. These sessions were part of the school's agreement with Callum's parents following the most recent school incident. It was either the sessions, or he risked expulsion.

"Okay, we'll come back to that," Yvonne said eventually relenting. "Tell me what you like to do… What did you do during the school holidays?"

"Went to London," Oliver replied.

"Okay, good, you went to London, who did you go with, and what did you see when you were there?"

"Tower of London," Oliver said into his chest, his muffled words barely legible.

"The Tower of London, wow, did your dad take you?"

There was no response, Oliver had frozen, his gaze was fixed straight ahead of him.

"Oliver?" Yvonne asked. "Are you okay?"

There was nothing in the way of a response, or even understanding from Oliver. Eventually, Yvonne followed the path of his gaze to see what he had become focused on. He appeared to be staring at a blinking orange light on her answering machine that was sitting on the sideboard behind her.

"What's the fascination with the orange light?" She asked.

In a split second, Oliver came around, as if snapped out of a trance.

"Oliver, are you okay? Are you happy to continue?" Yvonne asked.

Oliver shrugged and nodded, blissfully unaware of his lapse.

"And what did you see there, then?" Yvonne asked.

"Where?" Oliver asked, having lost his place in the conversation.

"In London, Oliver, you went to the Tower of London, what did you see there?" She asked.

"Where people got their heads cut off," Oliver replied.

"Ah, yes," Yvonne exclaimed, temporarily reminiscing about her last trip there many years before. "What else did you see?"

"The axes they used to do it," Oliver said with a wry smile emerging on his face.

"The actual axes?" Yvonne questioned.

"The *actual* axes," Oliver said proudly, sitting up in the wicker chair as he did so.

"Well, I'm sure over the years they've had to replace an axe head here, or a handle there, so probably not the original axe that had been used."

Yvonne was speaking flippantly, but even this was over Oliver's head. There was a long-running quip about the original axe that executed Mary Queen of Scots. Since the execution, it had had two replacement heads and three replacement handles, but was still considered the original axe. However, this was wasted on Oliver. Yvonne knew it was a poor attempt at livening the mood, but it was worth a try.

In an attempt to get off this morbid subject, Yvonne asked what else Oliver and his father did on their London trip.

"London Dungeons," Oliver said gleefully.

Yvonne sat wide-eyed. She felt this wasn't an appropriate venue for someone with such a fragile disposition, which Oliver undoubtedly had. "Whose idea was that?" she asked.

"Mine! We just happened to be walking past it, and I wanted to go inside," Oliver stated.

Yvonne wasn't entirely comfortable exploring this subject. But given that this was their first session together, building a rapport was much more important than the subject matter. Besides, such a topic could give a unique insight into Oliver's current state of mind, which could prove useful in future sessions. She decided to indulge him.

"So, what did you see, Oliver?" she asked.

"Oh, it was great," he replied, "there were people in makeup jumping out on you, and there was a really cool ride in there that really made me jump. But the best bit was all the horror. The ways they used to torture and kill people. Did you know they'd hang kids as young as me for stealing a loaf of bread a hundred years ago?"

"No, I didn't, is that true then?" Yvonne asked, trying not to devalue Oliver's expertise on the subject. Yvonne was actually well aware of the possibility having seen *Les Misérables*.

"It's true," he continued, "there's a whole list of things they'd hang you for back then: stealing a sheep, pickpocketing, housebreaking, whatever that is…"

"Burglary," Yvonne interjected to address the point, "burglary is the modern term for housebreaking."

"Ohhh, cheers for that," Oliver said. "Didn't like that bit, though, them hanging kids. There was a Court bit, and my dad offered me up for it. He was only messing, but it scared the shit out of me."

On hearing the expletive Yvonne started scribbling on her notepad. On seeing this, Oliver thought he had offended her and immediately offered an apology.

"Why did you feel the need to apologise, Oliver? Although, I'm glad you did, but why did you feel the need?" she asked.

"Coz I thought I'd upset you when you started scribbling. I thought maybe you were writing something bad about me. I don't like people thinking bad things about me."

Yvonne turned the pad so Oliver could see the notes for the session. Below the date and time, and Oliver's name were a couple of lines written from before the session. The most recent entry simply stated:

'Possibly doesn't like to cause offence or be centre of attention.'

Oliver saw that the comment had nothing to do with being foul-mouthed, or anything of a similar connotation. He sat back with an evident sense of relief. He smiled, Yvonne mirrored his sentiment. They continued.

There was a momentary pause as Oliver struggled to remember where he had left off on his earlier recollection of his trip to London. To lighten the situation, and further build on the rapport, Yvonne assisted him by saying. "You said the ride scared the *shit* out of you…" She intentionally overemphasised the expletive to provoke a positive reaction in Oliver.

"Oh, yeah," he smiled, "yeah, it did all right! It was amazing to see what people used to do to each other. It was nuts back then."

"Yes, it was, Oliver, in some respects it's a good thing that times have changed. Do you think they've gone too far the other way though?"

A look of confusion came over Oliver's face. Yvonne realised the terminology of her question was maybe a little too complex for Oliver. After all, despite his obvious intellectual ability and sensitivity, he *was* still only a nine-year-old boy. "Apologies, Oliver, allow me to rephrase my question. Do you feel that we are too easy on people who break the law nowadays? Do you feel things would be better off if there was a greater threat of punishment for breaking the law?"

Yvonne knew this was likely to cause a significant reaction in Oliver, and from her experience, retribution was a common factor in such cases. "Do you feel the punishment fits the crime these days, Oliver?"

Oliver sat back in his chair. His face displayed a maturity far beyond his years. His hands now clasped in front of his face, his eyes now looked to the floor in quiet contemplation. The top knuckle rubbing across his top lip. After a few seconds, his eyes raised to again make contact with Yvonne's. He started to shake his head.

Yvonne could see around his clasped hands that he was biting his top lip. Was this to stifle any attempt and need to cry? She didn't know, she couldn't tell, but most likely.

Oliver's eyes closed, in their action, like wringing out a sponge, a single tear was squeezed from each eye. Realising this, Oliver scrunched his eyes shut as if to draw the escaped tears back in, but without success.

Finally admitting defeat, he opened his eyes and reclaimed eye contact with Yvonne. He laid his hands in his lap and proudly displayed his face, now glistening with tears in the light shining through the slats of the blinds.

"Do I feel the punishment fits the crime?" he asked, confirming his understanding of the question before he offered any reply.

Yvonne sat resolute and nodded as she gave a single word reply, "Yes."

"I feel the punishment should match that of the crime," he said.

Chapter Five
Oliver, aged 13

"Mr Bennett, this is Constable Harvey, we spoke previously, when you attended the police station with Oliver a few months ago…"

"Ah yes, officer, what can I do for you?" Mr Bennett replied.

"Well, sir, I just wanted to advise you that Oliver is no longer connected with the offence for which he was arrested. We no longer need to reserve the right to speak to the two of you again on the subject."

"And why is that," Mr Bennett enquired, "what happened?"

"Well, sir, we currently have someone else on bail who *is* a forensic match to the blood sample found at the scene as we had discussed. As a result, we no longer need to consider Oliver as having had anything to do with this investigation."

"Well, I could've told you that weeks ago, but I'm happy you've been able to figure it out for yourselves," he said in a flippant reply.

After the events of the previous evening, this call did not come as a surprise at all.

oOo

The previous evening, after dinner, Oliver had suggested that they both sit down and watch a documentary on the medieval period on The History Channel. This wasn't something his father had an interest in at the moment, as he was focused on spreadsheets, bank statements and diaries, as he was getting a head start on his tax return. As usual, he had his papers strewn across the dining room table. The dining room adjoined the living room.

Oliver felt that his father wouldn't be interested in the documentary, and as he was busy at work, Oliver said he'd watch the programme in his room, so as not to be a distraction to his father. Although he *did* have an interest in the programme, in reality, it was merely an excuse for him to spend the remainder of the evening in his room.

"Have you done your homework?" his father asked him as he walked up the stairs.

"All done," came the now distant reply.

"Good lad," his father said. The only reply that earned was the sound of a door shutting upstairs.

oOo

With all the i's dotted, and the t's crossed, Paul Bennett started to make some order out of the chaos he had created. He began to tidy his work area so that it bore some resemblance to a dining room.

When all was neat, he wiped his brow with the sleeve of his shirt, before looking at his watch. It read 1.43 a.m.

"Shit!" he exclaimed. He realised that he had been working for over six hours without a break. But more importantly, he realised that he hadn't heard a peep from Oliver since he had gone upstairs to watch his documentary.

He got to his feet as best he could, his legs returning to life after having been dormant for so long. He didn't want to call up to Oliver, as he felt it likely that he would have settled himself down for the night. So, he casually walked to the bottom of the stairs before tiptoeing up them. Because his legs were still numb he had to rely on the bannister more than he'd have liked. The bannister creaked in unison with a floorboard which caused Paul to freeze. It was then he heard the sounds of the television coming from Oliver's room.

Paul made his way to Oliver's door and dropped the handle. He pushed the door open, hoping to see his son sprawled out on the bed, or face down on his desk asleep, having nodded off in the middle of the programme.

But, as Paul stood in the now fully open doorway, he was confronted with a scene no longer alien to him.

He looked across to see, as before, the window left ajar. To all intents and purposes it looked to be closed, but on closer inspection could be seen a gap large enough for fingers to pull the window open from the outside.

"Oh, for fuck's sake," he said as if there was someone there he intended to hear.

With a feeling of déjà vu, Paul went back downstairs. He then slipped on a jacket and his shoes, before returning to the dining room to pick up his mobile phone from the dining room table.

Just as he was about to open the front door to leave, he heard noises coming from upstairs, from Oliver's room.

Paul walked to the bottom of the stairs. He waited, and he listened. He didn't have line of sight on Oliver's bedroom door, so all he could do was just listen. He didn't want to attempt to ascend the stairs in case the creaky bannister or stairs gave him away, so he just listened.

There were nondescript noises coming from Oliver's room. Nothing to raise any alarms or concern with Paul, nothing compelling him to go rushing up the stairs and burst into his son's bedroom. So, he continued to wait and listen. He looked at his watch, it now read 2.08 a.m.

After what felt like a couple of minutes, the door to Oliver's bedroom opened. There were a couple of creaks as footsteps ventured out onto the landing. The light and TV must've been turned off because there was no illumination to the hallway. Then there was an audible click and the landing lit up. The bathroom light had been turned on. This still didn't cause Paul any real concern.

He stood there patiently, he was expecting to hear the toilet flush before further activity on the landing. But no, instead he heard the shower being turned on. Loud at first as the cascade hit the bath below, but after a few seconds if became muffled indicating that someone, Oliver, had stepped under it.

Using this to disguise his own movements, Paul took off his jacket and hung it on the bannister, normally he hated this practice, but needs must now. He kicked off his shoes and pushed them to one side. He then ascended the stairs.

The shower was now in full flow. He had to be quick. He walked into Oliver's room which was now in darkness, he closed the door behind him, as he had found it. As he manoeuvred across the room he felt his feet get caught on something. It felt like discarded clothes, but he couldn't be sure in the darkness. He would have to wait for that answer. He sat himself down on the bed to await his son's return. From where he sat, Paul could hear the shower running. He would have plenty of warning before his son would re-enter his room.

It wasn't long before he heard the shower being turned off. *'Any moment now,'* Paul thought. He had concluded that what he had kicked was most likely Oliver's clothing, so he must've walked across to the bathroom naked, or at the very least in his underwear.

Then he heard the same click again. Paul looked at the gap around the bedroom door. The glow had gone, the bathroom light was now out. Any moment now. Paul started to squint to pre-empt the bedroom lights being turned on. But nothing, not yet.

It was then he heard footsteps on the stairs. This didn't make sense, and started to cause confusion. Then this conundrum also had its answer. Paul heard the washing machine start up. Now Paul was concerned. First a shower, now washing his clothes, what had Oliver been up to?

Time passed even slower now as Paul waited in the dark for his son to come back up the stairs. He contemplated leaving his son's bedroom and going back downstairs to see what Oliver was doing, and was in the process of standing back up when he heard the stair-boards creak again. Then the bedroom door was pushed back, and in an instant the room was illuminated.

"Fucking hell, Dad, you scared the shit out of me!" Oliver exclaimed at seeing the figure of his father sat on his bed.

Once Paul's eyes had adjusted to the light, he could see his son stood in the open doorway. He was dressed in a t-shirt and joggers and was holding a packet of biscuits.

"Fucking hell, Dad?" Paul questioned. "I should be saying something along those lines, what the hell have you been doing? Where have you been that needs you to take a shower and wash your clothes the second you get in?"

He then remembered tripping over something on Oliver's floor when he first came in. He looked down to see what it was.

All Paul could see was a supermarket carrier bag that had been knotted shut, he couldn't make out what was concealed within. "What's this?" he added to his increasingly long list of unanswered questions.

"You'd better start coming up with some answers for me, or do I need to call the cops?" he said, giving the ultimatum.

Admitting defeat, Oliver gestured with his hands for his father to calm down. His father also gestured for Oliver to join him sitting on the bed. Oliver felt more articulate when he was standing and able to move and express himself freely, so he remained standing. He started to pace around the bedroom as he began to recount the events of the evening for his father.

oOo

After Oliver had duped his father into thinking he was going upstairs to watch the documentary, he had sneaked out much like he had on numerous occasions since being made aware of the cat ripper by the police on the occasion of his arrest.

He hadn't known about these attacks until the police had told him. But what he was told, in their attempts to disgust his father into giving permission for them to take his blood, appalled them both. They had been given explicit details of the incidents to that date.

As a result, Oliver left the police station sickened about the crimes, and worse still that people could believe *him* capable of them. It was from that moment he felt compelled to act. He wanted to, in whatever capacity he could, contribute to the efforts to identify the culprit.

Oliver had been reading local articles in the newspapers and online. From these, he was able to deduce that the attacks were happening on weekdays only. The time-frame was less specific as the attacks were only being discovered the following morning. As a result, and in order to avoid drawing attention to himself either at home or in public, Oliver was going out two or three times each week between midnight and four o'clock.

Oliver had been making careful notes of everyone he had seen when he was out on each occasion. From the news, he was able to determine on what dates attacks had taken place. He was then able to deduce who was out on the nights in question. From his notes, this identified one person who appeared to have no purpose for being out. As it turned out, Oliver had seen this individual out on occasions other than the attacks. But he deduced that on those nights he had failed in his task, and had gone home disappointed and frustrated.

Frustrated, possibly because the attacks were becoming ever more frenzied. Oliver likened him to Jack the Ripper, his killings appeared to be more frenzied as time went on, and on the one occasion where he was foiled in his devilish deed, his next victim ultimately paid the price.

Oliver even had an idea of where this person lived. He had become the sole focus of Oliver's patrols until he was ruled out, or someone else made themselves prominent.

He was much bigger than Oliver, but Oliver still believed him to be a teenager, maybe twenty at an absolute stretch. So, any attack Oliver would make to subdue him would need to be an ambush as opposed to a confrontation, and Oliver felt he knew the best place for this to take place. The only aspect that hadn't occurred to him was how to identify this person to the police without involving or potentially implicating himself.

The only way he felt he could do this was to allow another pet to be targeted, to potentially allow another owner to be devastated. This way Oliver could be sure of two things; firstly, that this person was the culprit, and secondly, that he was carrying evidence of the most recent attacks when Oliver chose to strike.

Oliver's last few excursions were fruitless. He would sit in wait outside the house for his target to emerge. But, he had timed it perfectly this time. It felt like a mere matter of minutes, as he waited in position, when he saw his target walk from the house.

Oliver kept a safe distance as he followed behind him. He was small and dressed all in black, so he blended seamlessly into the shadows. Oliver's target favoured the alleyways as opposed to the streets to get around. This was probably why the police patrols hadn't found him.

Despite the distance he kept behind him, Oliver could hear his target calling out, presumably to cats. Oliver could also hear a gravelly sound, as if he were shaking cat treats or food to entice his unsuspecting prey to think of him as friendly.

"What a fucking wanker," Oliver whispered to himself at his drawn conclusions.

Oliver walked along one side of a long residential road. He was about twenty yards behind his target, and on the other side of the road, when he saw him stop and crouch down. Oliver closed in on him as far as the shadows would allow him.

Oliver then withdrew an object from his sleeve. He had concealed a rounders bat up his sleeve. This is similar in appearance, yet much smaller than a baseball bat, but conversely much easier to conceal and wield with one hand.

From where Oliver now stood, he could see the house in front of which his target now stood. He could also see the reason he stopped there and had crouched down. An all-white cat was lurking under a car on the driveway, and he was calling to it in attempts to get it to come out to him. He had one hand extended; Oliver thought that maybe it had some sort of treat in it. The bottom line for Oliver was that he was distracted. That's all Oliver wanted and needed right now.

So many things were going through Oliver's mind right now; should he just shout out, and scare the cat off, and foil the attacker just to allow him to strike another day? Or, must he risk another animal's life, and more misery to try to thwart him now, tonight. No one else had come this close, and the information he had would be useless if he just handed it to the police. Now was the time to act.

Oliver side-stepped along the pavement, never taking his eyes of the crouched figure across from him. Beyond this figure he could, however, now see the emerging shape of a curious feline.

The crouched figure remained static as Oliver and the feline closed in on him from opposite sides. Oliver hoped for no cars to come past as he made his way across the road, the feline hoped for treats.

Oliver had timed his approach perfectly, he would reach his target at the same time as the cat, until the feline's appetite got the better of him and ran the last few feet. Oliver could no longer see the cat as the crouched figure completely obscured his view. But he knew the cat was still there, because all of his attention was on a spot directly in front of him.

Oliver was only a matter of feet behind the crouched figure now. He had the element of surprise he would need in order to overcome the larger and potentially stronger opponent.

Then, in an instant, the crouched figure lurched forward, placing one hand on the ground and reaching out with the other.

There was a cry from the cat as it was grabbed. Oliver could hear spitting and hissing coming from beyond the silhouetted figure.

The figure was momentarily unbalanced as he had to reach beyond his grasp to grab the cat. As he regained posture, Oliver knew this was his time to strike. He felt that at any moment the ripper would deal a fatal blow to the wretched creature.

Oliver stepped to the left of the figure and swung the bat against the elbow of the arm that was resting on the ground and taking the figure's bodyweight. In an instant, the elbow buckled and the figure fell to the ground. He screamed in agony as his weight fell on the now broken joint. He then threw himself onto his back to take the weight off his arm in an attempt to alleviate the pain.

The downed figure looked up at Oliver, but his face was encapsulated in shadows, rendering it unrecognisable. Realising what was happening, the figure started to stand up, doing his best to not use the damaged limb. Oliver assessed his opponent, he was bigger than first impressions would suggest. He then realised if he got to his feet he wouldn't stand a chance against him one-on-one.

Oliver had to keep him on the ground. He saw his chance, and he took it. He brought the bat down on the prone figure's bent leg, impacting the kneecap itself. There was another scream of pain. Lights were turning on in the house. The culprit could no longer make any attempts to stand, and resigned himself to the ground battle.

To ensure the occupants of the house came outside, Oliver looked around him for something to throw at the house. He found a golf ball sized stone. He picked it up and threw it at one of the windows that had a light on. The outer pane smashed. Oliver prayed this would have the desired effect of bringing the occupants running outside.

Oliver retreated, he ran back across the road, back into the shadows that had afforded him protection only moments earlier. His heart beating so fast he felt it would escape his chest.

From his vantage point, Oliver could see the occupants coming out from inside the house. They could be seen to approach the downed figure on their driveway. Oliver physically had his fingers crossed that they would realise the situation, detain him and call the police.

One of the occupants, a middle-aged burly man in his pyjamas, grabbed hold of the figure beneath him. Oliver was confident he would do the right thing. Any touch the man made resulted in a scream of pain. There was no compassion.

A woman rushed up to them, she picked up the motionless cat. Having scooped it up in her arms she rushed back into the house, narrowly squeezing by a younger man who was on the phone as he came outside and went towards the screams on the driveway.

Oliver realised he didn't need to be there any more. There was nothing more to see, and certainly nothing more he needed to do. He kept to the shadows and began retracing his steps. But what to do with the bat. Should he take it home, or dump it? He thought it best to take it home and dispose of it properly there.

When he got back home he sneaked back in through his window. Once back in the safety of his bedroom he stripped off his jacket and dropped it on the floor, still with the bat concealed within one of the sleeves. This landed on the carpeted floor with a dull thud.

Oliver then grabbed his nightwear from on top of his pillow. Then before reaching for the bedroom door, he turned off the TV that had been playing to itself for the last hour or so, before crossing the hallway into the bathroom.

oOo

"And the rest you know, Dad," said Oliver, concluding his story.

Realising that it had been the jacket and bat that he had kicked when first entering his room, his father sat on the edge of Oliver's bed silently nodding as if compiling a plan.

"Okay," he began, "forget about washing anything, we need to burn it, yeah, and I mean everything, even your trainers."

This revelation from his father shocked him. He had just admitted to his father that he had beaten someone with a rounders bat, and now his father was deciding how best to conceal the crime. After a moment Oliver began nodding along enthusiastically.

"We won't do anything tonight, it will look too obvious, but we'll bag it up for now, and I'll get rid of it all tomorrow. Right, for now give it all to me, and then you get yourself some sleep. You've got school in the morning, and I don't want you looking like you've been up half the night. And give me those biscuits."

Paul picked up the jacket from the floor. He could now feel the bat concealed down one sleeve. Clutching it to his chest, he pulled back the quilt for Oliver to slip under. He then kissed his son on his forehead and headed towards the door, he turned the light off and closed the bedroom door behind him.

Chapter Six
Oliver, aged 17

"Well, Oliver, this is our last session together. I wanted to begin by reviewing the progress you feel you've made in the time we've been together. How do you feel you have benefited from these sessions?"

"I dunno?" came Oliver's reply, slouching in his chair and appearing generally uninterested.

No longer was Yvonne sitting across from Oliver in these sessions. She specialised in adolescents, and her area of expertise ceased some time ago when it came to Oliver. She hadn't been his therapist for some time, long since the baton had been passed to someone who was better practiced in dealing with traumatised juveniles.

Oliver had been in and out of counselling since he was nine years old, since his emotions began to manifest themselves physically. Nine was considered too early by conventional standards, but attempts had to be made to kerb Oliver's behaviour before it got out of hand.

For the last eighteen plus months Oliver had been seeing his current therapist, Gerald Wilcox. He specialised in juvenile's who had experienced severe childhood trauma.

A core focus of their sessions was to piece together the exact details of the trigger event. In Oliver's case, the tragic night that his mother was taken from him. This was initially done by Oliver giving his best recollection of the events, which in turn was added to, and prompted by the police reports to help fill in certain blanks.

The object of this was to give Oliver the fullest picture possible in order to minimise the times where his own mind would fill in the blanks for himself, which used to result in exaggerated emotion, usually manifested in anger. With understanding, it was hoped would come an eventual acceptance and tolerance.

"I can accept that, what I'd like to do today, is for you to recount for me in as much detail as possible what you can recall about that night. When we first started discussing it your recollection was fragmented, but we've done a lot of work since then. So today, I'd like you to give me the fullest account possible." There was a pause. "Do you feel you could do that?"

Oliver sat up, a look of defiant determination came across his face. As painful as this was going to be, he wanted to achieve this, as this was what was fuelling so much emotion and pain for him.

"In your own time then, Oliver," Gerald prompted.

"It was late in the evening, it was dark…" Oliver began.

oOo

Oliver had spent the afternoon after school in the care of his grandparents, as both his parents were at work. The arrangement was that whichever parent finished work first, would let the other one know that they would be collecting Oliver and take him home.

On this occasion, Mary, Oliver's mother finished work first. She worked as a pensions manager for a large multi-national electronics company. As a result, similar to Paul, who was an independent contractor, it was impossible to know exactly when they would finish work on any given day. They didn't have the luxury of being bound by the traditional nine-to-five mentality. If things weren't finished by the end of the working day, they were required to finish them. Added to which insult, they would frequently watch their underlings leave work, whilst they had to stay to pick up the slack that had been dropped during the day.

It was an autumnal evening, a Thursday. Mary finished work only slightly later than usual, and in the last hour or so she kept checking her mobile phone, hoping to see a message from Paul to say he'd already finished and would be collecting Oliver. But alas, no message was seen.

Right up until she had shut down her computer, having left her office and was walking to her car, she remained hopeful of receiving news from Paul. Still nothing.

It was only when she was sat in her car with her seatbelt on and the key in the ignition did she accept her fate and send those all-important messages. Mary drove a small five-door hatchback. It wasn't anything special, several years old, and rather tatty, but it suited her needs perfectly. Although the boot space was on the small side, especially if she had groceries as well as everything she needed for Oliver.

The first message was sent to Paul, it read:

'Just finished, I'll get Ollie, I do need to swing by the shops on the way for a few things x'

Then to her mother:

'Leaving now, see you shortly x'

The drive from her office to her parents would normally take about twenty-five minutes. But due to roadworks and the need to stop for a few bits and pieces from the supermarket, it was nearly double that when she pulled up outside her parents' house.

Mary rushed out of the car and disappeared into her parents' home. She emerged a few minutes later with Oliver. He had been asleep immediately prior to her arrival and was bleary-eyed and disorientated as she led him to the car.

It was a cold evening, so Mary had the heating on for Oliver's benefit, but this made her feel uncomfortably warm. She began to wish she'd taken her coat off before heading home. For a moment, she weighed up the options of pulling over for a moment to remove her coat, or simply opening the window. After a moment of silent debate, the window option won.

The route between Mary's home and her parents was a fast route, but it consisted mainly of unlit country roads. The nuisance of the roadworks was now behind her, and she was making fairly good time. Oliver had nodded off again soon after departure and had yet to stir in the child seat behind her.

He was secured directly behind her, as opposed to being a nearside passenger, as she had once read that the safest place in a car is directly behind the driver. It had been statistically proven that drivers will subconsciously and inadvertently protect themselves in an accident, and that their final actions will be ones to avoid danger, even if this placed other occupants of their vehicle in harm's way. So, the seat directly behind the driver was statistically the safest place to be, and hence the safest place for Oliver. Mary's interior mirror had been adjusted to show Oliver instead of out of the rear window.

Because Mary was able to maintain the speed limit throughout this part of the route she was making good time. However, the trade-off was excessive wind noise coming from the open window. Time to reassess her options. Mary felt she had to close the window, because she didn't want the wind noise to wake Oliver. Mary closed the window.

The car started to warm up to an uncomfortable level for her again, *'nearly home,'* she thought.

It was then that her mobile phone buzzed in its cradle on the dashboard. She afforded herself a glance across at it.

It was a message from Paul, it read: 'I'm home.'

"I'm home," she said to herself. "I'm home. Bloody hell! What about the *I'm leaving now* and *I'll get Ollie?* I'll give you I'm bloody home!"

Mary could feel a heat rising up her neck, she was angry that their well laid and practised agreement had been abused. She became angrier and angrier with the situation as time went by, and she felt herself getting hotter and hotter. To such an extent that it began to cloud her concentration. As a result, she misjudged a couple of corners and had to snatch at the steering to avoid close encounters with the verge.

As she rounded a corner, her headlights picked up the road sign indicating a lay-by a short distance ahead. It was still on an unlit stretch of road. Not the best idea at this time of night, but all she was going to do would be to take off her coat and that would be it.

Although there was not another vehicle on the road, Mary indicated to pull across the carriageway into the lay-by. It was an unmade surface, with lots of loose gravel, so braking from the speed she had been travelling at caused some skidding as she came to a halt.

Once stationary, Mary alighted from her car without turning the engine off or even cancelling the indicator. As it turned out, it wasn't such a swift action of taking off her coat, chucking it in the boot, or backseat next to Oliver, before heading off again.

She was still angry with Paul, and with the situation as it was, she felt she needed to allow herself a moment or two to calm down before continuing their journey home.

She stood a few steps away from the car, the driver's door still open. She paced back and forth, dragging her feet in the loose gravel.

She felt she needed to pacify this situation, and lay the groundwork for when she got home. Mary reached inside the car and retrieved her mobile phone from the dashboard cradle. As she stood up again, she began scrolling through her contact list and phoned *home*.

"Yeah, hi, sweetie, it's only me." She paused to allow Paul time to reply, she continued, "Yeah, I'm on my way home now, I'm wondering if you can just start doing dinner, we're about twenty minutes away, anything you want, would be nice to have it already on the go for when we get in, okay? Love you, bye."

Mary reached inside the door and put her phone on top of the dashboard, she would replace it in the cradle once she had sat down again. But not just yet, first things first.

The reason she had stopped in the first place was to take her coat off, this had yet to be done. She was about twenty minutes from home, that was the truth, but it would be an uncomfortable twenty minutes if she didn't take care of this first.

As Mary walked around the back of the car she began slipping the coat off her shoulders, so, by the time she stood in front of the hatchback tailgate the coat was in her arms. Mary lifted the tailgate and laid her coat on top of the grocery bags, she glanced over the parcel shelf into the back seat of the car. She could see Oliver stirring in his child seat.

As it turned out this would be the last time she would ever see her son.

As Mary brought the tailgate down, she felt a firm tug on her ponytail. This grip wrenched her head back causing her severe pain. She screamed. But her screams were short-lived as the hand that pulled her head back then brought it crashing forward and down into the tailgate, which stunned Mary.

Did she lose consciousness at this point? No one knows.

Oliver was woken by the increasingly distant screams of his mother. As a result of her screams and finding himself alone, he struggled in attempts to free himself from the child seat. He frantically tried to release the straps, without success. Then he screamed and called for his mother. The only light he could see was the interior light of the car which was still illuminated as the driver's door remained open, all around it was blackness. There was nothing else to be seen, only heard, and all that could be heard were screams; Oliver's screams in competition with his mother's screams.

Then, there were only Oliver's screams, and when he stopped, all that remained was silence.

Then there was another sound, to Oliver it didn't compute, to him it was unrecognisable. But it was the sound of heavy shoes or work boots on gravel. The noise was getting louder, it was coming closer.

A figure then emerged at the driver's door, then started to sit down in the driver's seat. Oliver called out, "Mommy."

The figure froze. From the stench that emanated from it, Oliver didn't know this person. The figure then cautiously got back out of the car. For a moment, there was silence.

Then all of a sudden there was a face pressed against Oliver's window, intermittently glowing orange from the offside indicator. This face frightened Oliver, he started to scream again.

Then, after a moment he was gone. Again, there was nothing but silence and solitude.

Then, a chilling breeze came over the top of Oliver's head, this confused him until he realised that the tailgate had been lifted, before a deafening thud stopped it as the tailgate came crashing back down.

Finally, there was an uninterrupted silence, broken only occasionally with a whimper from Oliver as the darkness consumed him. The engine had now been turned off, and the keys taken from the ignition, as well as the boot being rummaged before the face at the window had run off into the darkness.

The face at the window, the face seen only briefly, for a single moment in time, but a face he would never forget.

oOo

"Then the police found me, they said between the call Mum made to my dad and them finding me, was about an hour," Oliver said.

Gerald sat in silence, aghast at the account that Oliver had recited to him. Concerned by the lack of emotion and empathy he had for his younger self. He was witnessing complete detachment from the situation, as if Oliver was reading a fictitious account as opposed to an actual incident he, himself, had lived through.

"Then they found Mum, she was about twenty yards away from me, in the woods, she was dead. She'd been beaten and raped, left to die."

"Do you know how they found *him*, Oliver?" Gerald asked referring to Mary's attacker.

"Yeah, the police said they'd found things on Mum that he'd left behind, and also his fingerprints were all over the car, the window and where he'd touched things. They said he was stupid to do what he did, he made it too easy for them to catch him."

"And how do you feel about the sentence they gave him? Do you feel that he deserved fifteen years in prison?"

"It's what the law says he deserves, if they say he should get fifteen years, then he deserves to get fifteen years!"

"That's not what I asked, Oliver," Gerald said.

"I know what you asked, what do you want me to say? Do you want me to say that every night I imagine seeing him punished, that every night I imagine doing it myself? Is that what you want to hear?" Oliver paused. "Well, I'm sorry to disappoint you, but that's not what I imagine at all."

"How is your father coping with things?" Gerald then asked.

"Same as always, he'd rather talk to the bottom of a bottle than to me, hardly an evening goes by where he doesn't have a drink nowadays."

"Try not to judge him, Oliver, we all have our individual coping mechanisms. Your father has just chosen a less healthy and productive method. What coping mechanisms have you adopted, Oliver?"

"Me? I just look to the future, have to, sure as hell can't change the past," Oliver replied.

Chapter Seven
Oliver, aged 18

"Happy Birthday, Son," Paul Bennett said, as his son sat down to breakfast. He slid a card and a small gift-wrapped box across the table to where Oliver sat. "Your mother would've been proud of the man you've grown into."

His father's closing sentiment suddenly made this moment bittersweet for Oliver. In an instant, in a single word, the joy of today was washed away in a torrent of painful memories.

Try as he might, Oliver found the moment overwhelming, and he wept tears for his mother. His father, seeing Oliver's reaction realised his mistake. All he wanted was to include his beloved wife somewhere in today's celebration. But even the mere mention of her was still so very painful for them both. Especially on a monumental occasion such as their only child's coming of age. After a few minutes, after they had both taken sufficient time to pay their respects, the conversation came back to the moment.

Oliver opened the card first. He'd always been told it was proper etiquette to open the card first, to acknowledge the sender of the gift before devoting attention to the gift itself. Then to the gift, it was a small package. As Oliver handled it, he could hear a metal-on-metal rattle come from within. *What was it?* he thought.

He peeled away the outer layer of gift wrapping paper to reveal a jewellery box. It wasn't a brand-new box; the corners were scuffed, and the maroon leather had faded over time. It had evidently come into his father's possession by other means, and he was recycling it here.

Oliver rotated the box in his hands to ensure it was the right way up, and that the hinges were away from him. He opened the lid. Inside was the answer to what had been rattling. Inside was a single key on a key-ring. Like the jewellery box, the key was old and worn, it was a car key. It certainly wasn't a key to a brand-new car. Oliver picked up the key and set the box back on the table between them. It was a VW key, Oliver held the key in his open palm, the key-ring pendant swung off the side of his hand. Oliver steadied the pendant and examined it.

The pendant was a capital letter 'M', it was about two inches tall and made of metal. This meant it had a significant weight to it. Oliver's instinct was to clench his fist around the key to allow the pendant to be held rigidly protruding from the underside of his fist. He then made a stabbing motion down towards the table. His father did notice the aggression in this action.

"She's parked outside," his father interjected, feeling he needed to refocus the conversation, "*she may not look like much but she's got it where it counts.*"

Oliver looked up wide-eyed, he smiled. It was funny for him to hear his dad spout movie quotes in everyday conversation. One of the pastimes they shared together was their love of movies, and they would quite often find themselves in front of the TV of an evening, or at the cinema together.

"I haven't got much on today, so why don't you take me for a spin in it later, we can find a nice pub somewhere now you're old enough, I'll buy you a birthday lunch?"

Oliver's eyes had reverted to the key-ring pendant, the letter 'M' which was as battered at the key and the jewellery box. This key-ring was his mother's, and the 'M' stood for Mary, his mother.

As suggested, after breakfast Oliver took his father for a spin in his new car, and his father, in turn, took him for lunch. This was the first time Oliver ever drove his father.

Chapter Eight
Oliver, aged 17

"Evening, you've got an assault victim in here somewhere," a police officer said having approached the nurse's station within the accident and emergency department of the local hospital.

The nurse looked up, made eye contact with the officer leaning over the counter between them, but with a somewhat bewildered look on her face. She turned to her colleague who had just got off the phone. "Marie, assault victim?"

Marie initially shared her colleague's bewilderment before the penny dropped. "Oh, yeah, assault victim, bay nine, Garry Yarnton. He doesn't know you guys have been called. He says he's been assaulted, refuses to say exactly what happened, or by whom. He's definitely been beaten though."

"Yarnton? Oh yeah, I know him. Thanks," came the reply from the officer.

"Oh," Marie then exclaimed, as she recalled a further detail that was pertinent, "he's also been branded."

The look of bewilderment was now shared by the officer as he turned and walked off in the direction of the treatment bays, followed closely by his colleague. The officer was familiar with the department having attended the hospital for previous incidents. He didn't need to be given directions by hospital staff.

When they reached bay nine the curtains were drawn, whoever was on the other side either wanted privacy or was undergoing treatment. The officer listened closely for sounds from within the bay. He could hear a muffled conversation, so he deduced it was the latter, the occupant was most likely undergoing treatment.

After what was in reality no longer than a minute or two, the curtains were drawn back. Two people emerged from the bay, one was a nurse, the other in scrubs. At this hospital, like so many others, the colour of the scrubs denoted their role, in this case they were maroon. The officer was none the wiser as to the relevance that had.

Seeing the officers, the medical staff gave a welcoming gesture, but without a specific indication that they wanted to talk, they didn't break their stride and carried on past

With the curtains now fully back, the patient could clearly see the police officers outside of his bay. He had no doubt in his mind that they were there to see him. The officers looked in, and they could see that the discomfort the patient was feeling probably went far beyond the physical pain he was enduring.

To the police, Yarnton is what was known as a prolific or persistent offender. Most of the officers who worked that area had some dealings with him at one time or another. He was usually a prime suspect in most acquisitive crime. So much so, that crime trends were based on whether or not he was inside at any given time. But to the officers he was just a *shit-bag*.

The officers stood at the foot of his trolley bed looking up at him. The patient was obviously in a great deal of physical pain, he had dressings on both hands, and another on his left cheek. Normally, this sort of sight would have curried sympathy from the officers towards a victim of crime. But when it was someone like Yarnton on the receiving end, it would give them cause to smile. Call it fate, call it karma, call it restorative justice, this was a sight frontline officers regaled in. They considered it payback for the blighted lives the likes of Yarnton had caused for countless others.

The first officer checked his watch to verify the time. He was on a night shift, so he wanted to make sure his greeting was time-accurate. "Good morning, Garry," he said gleefully.

"What's so fucking *good* about it?" came the response. The officer really didn't want to tell him, so he kept quiet and enjoyed the moment.

"Who have you been pissing off then?" he asked.

"I ain't been pissing off nobody," Yarnton replied. "I got jumped, now why ain't you guys out there finding this prick?"

"C'mon, Garry, I know *you* know how this works, I've got to ask you questions for you to tell me exactly what happened, *then* I've got to talk to the staff and find out about the injuries you've sustained, so *if* I do find someone responsible for this I know what to arrest them f…"

Yarnton interrupted the officer before he could finish. "Injuries? *Injuries*? I'll show you my *fucking* injuries!"

He reached up to his face with his bandaged hands and started to tease at the corners of the dressing covering his left cheek. He began to get frustrated as he couldn't lift a corner to get a good enough hold on it.

As his frustration grew, so did the pressure on his face, and as a result the wound started weeping again, which was becoming evident through the dressing. Eventually, Yarnton lifted a corner and ripped the dressing from his face in one swift move. This made both officers wince. He was now sitting up, breathing heavily and clearly agitated. "There, have a look, there's my *fucking* injuries."

The first officer stepped along the side of the trolley bed to get a closer look. The second officer had a brief look around the department, given Yarnton's outburst, before following his colleague.

All the other injuries that Yarnton had sustained were consistent with a fight, or a physical assault. His hands had dressings on them, the wounds couldn't be seen, but beneath them would be the suspected abrasion and impact injuries of a confrontation. Yarnton's face was swollen and bruised suggesting he had taken some blows to the face.

But the dressing on his cheek was covering a wound neither officer was expecting. Covering the entire left cheek, as obvious on his face as his nose, was the letter 'T', it wasn't an incision injury. It was as the nurse had forewarned them. Yarnton had the letter 'T' branded into his face. Due to his efforts to remove the dressing the wound had started to ooze, but beneath that the letter was clearly defined.

Due to Yarnton's outburst, and the resultant effect on the wound, the second officer had left the bay to ask hospital staff to re-attend the patient.

The first officer leaned over to get a closer look. He had no specific medical training, other than the basic first aid training given to all police officers, but he could see that this wound was deep. He felt with any more pressure or duration then it could've burnt through into the mouth cavity. Yarnton would be permanently scarred.

"So," the officer began, "are you gonna tell me what happened?"

"I ain't no grass, I ain't saying *shit*," Yarnton replied. He was now looking less defiant, and more distressed.

The officer stood back, away from the bed as he saw his colleague and hospital staff come into view. The officers congregated away from the trolley bed so as not to impede the nurses.

For the first time, the second officer was able to properly see the facial wound, he grimaced as he sucked through his teeth. "Ouch!" he eventually remarked, "that's a GBH any day of the week. Do you think he'll talk to us?"

"Not so far, said he *ain't no grass*. We'll get photos once they've cleaned him up, and we'll have to seize his clothing in case of any forensics, but without an account, description, or *even* a location where this took place we'll never really know what happened."

Without knowing exactly when or where an incident took place, it would be impossible for the police to review what could be thousands of hours of CCTV footage on the off-chance they may get lucky. Yarnton had made his own way to hospital, so without his co-operation, or any witnesses, it would be impossible to know the location of the incident. Had an ambulance attended, at least the police could narrow down the possible location and time frame to that of the call.

"So, if we don't get a forensics hit, it'll be case closed," the first officer said.

They both watched from just outside of the bay as the nurses cleaned up the facial wound. "Can I get a photograph before you dress it?" the first officer asked.

"Give us a minute, will ya," one of the nurses protested, as if feeling hassled and hurried by the police. This wasn't the case at all. Given the manic shift going on outside of the hospital, evident only to the officers by the radio messages they were hearing on their ear-pieces, they were happy for this to take as long as possible.

"Do you want a coffee?" the second officer asked.

71

"Yep, we're gonna be here a while, may as well make ourselves comfortable," he paused, "tell you what, whilst you're out there, best grab some paper evidence bags from the car so we can seize his clothing."

The second officer nodded his approval and left in the direction of the nurses' station.

oOo

After about ten minutes the officer returned. He was carrying a coffee in each hand, and what would look from a distance to be a rolled-up newspaper under his arm. In reality, this was a number of paper evidence bags as suggested.

"Cheers for that," the first officer said as he stood up from the chairs he had sourced for himself and his colleague in his absence. He initially took hold of both coffees to allow the second officer to sort himself out and take his seat. He was then handed back his coffee and they both sat.

Yarnton was now asleep, or at least he appeared to be. He had a fresh dressing on his face. It had already started to turn yellow in the middle as discharge still oozed from his facial wound.

After they had both finished their coffees, they started to sort out what they needed to seize from Yarnton's clothing. As per standard procedure, hand swabs and relevant clothing needed to be seized for all incidents of grievous bodily harm where it was suspected that one party came into physical contact with another. It wasn't necessary in *every* case, such as using a vehicle to cause the damage, or in the event of a shooting.

However, in this case it was relevant. As a result, Yarnton's outer clothing would be seized. This would include his jacket, trousers and footwear. This had been anticipated, so the second officer had brought only the required number of evidence bags. He brought four, one for the jacket, another for the trousers, and one for each of the shoes. The shoes were packaged separately to avoid cross-contamination, what could be on one shoe but not the other could determine how an element of the incident had actually taken place.

The clothing was searched prior to being packaged. This involved going through the pockets, and checking the lining was intact before placing it in the evidence bag. Yarnton's personal possessions, such as his wallet, keys and mobile phone, were placed in a separate bag for safekeeping for him.

It was as this was taking place that the second officer found in one of the outer jacket pockets a folded piece of paper. Initially, this was considered to be a drug wrap. It was common practice to deal powdered drugs in folded lottery tickets. But it was immediately obvious that this was not a lottery ticket. It was a piece of plain paper.

The officer slowly and carefully unfolded the piece of paper. At every fold, he ensured the opening was uppermost, so should there be any contents it would be held within the paper and not spilled. But there were no contents to be found. Only an equation handwritten on the inside of a fold.

T = Thief

To the second officer this didn't mean a great deal. He flipped the paper over to see if there was anything printed or written on the reverse, it was blank.

He then showed it to his colleague. "What do you make of this?" he asked.

When the first officer saw it, his eyes opened wide in surprise. He went to the pocket of his body armour and quickly got out his data terminal. He was in such a hurry he couldn't make his fingerprint unlock the device, having to resort to a password input.

Once unlocked, he went to the device's photo gallery. He then scrolled through the last few images of Yarnton until he got to the shot of his facial injury.

He showed this image to his colleague. He said one thing as he did so, "Tee!"

They then held the piece of paper next to the photograph to compare their findings.

No one said a word.

Chapter Nine
Present Day – Oliver, aged 19

"And lastly, I'd like to welcome Oliver to the team, I'll be crewing you with Dave for the duration of your tutor phase, okay?" the duty Sergeant said. This concluded the morning briefing.

As the team were dismissed, and in the process of leaving the briefing room, the Sergeant called back to Oliver, "Once you and Dave have signed-on to your car, can I see you in my office, there's a few things we need to go through?"

Oliver acknowledged the request, he then had to hurry to catch up with Dave, his colleague and mentor for his first ten weeks on patrol following his initial police training.

oOo

After readying their car, and checking all the equipment for the shift, Oliver attended the Sergeant's office as he had been requested. The purpose of this meeting was to allow a fuller introduction between PC Oliver Bennett and his immediate supervisor, as well as instructing him on a number of operational points that aren't readily taught in training school.

"Lastly, Oliver, it will probably not come as a surprise to you, but I am aware of what you've been through, as a result, Occ

Health have asked that you not be deployed to certain incidents for the time being. I'm sure you know what this means, without me going into greater detail? As a tutor unit, Dave has a certain discretion as to what incidents you go to, what's needed for your development. He's aware of this too, so it's nothing you have to worry about."

Oliver looked at his feet and shook his head, and despite the words being muffled and directed at the floor, his Sergeant heard them clearly "For fuck's sake," he said.

"Something you wanna say, Oliver?" his Sergeant challenged at hearing his insolent and disrespectful reply.

"Sarge, I don't *mean* to be disrespectful," Oliver began with a prepared response having anticipated this eventuality. "I had the same bullshit treatment at training school. I mean why, for Christ's sake? I can't be pampered forever, what happens if I keep getting protected now, and then all of a sudden, I'm dumped on one on my own with no experience? Surely, it's better for everyone to have me being mentored when I first get a griefy one, y'know, so they can keep an eye on me."

His Sergeant could certainly see Oliver's logic, but he was not prepared to overturn a recommendation as laid down by the Force's Occupational Health Unit. "I can see where you're coming from, Oliver, but that's how it's gonna be until further notice. Are we going to have a problem on the subject?"

"No, Sarge," said Oliver reassuringly.

"Okay, well if that's it, we're done," his Sergeant said.

Oliver nodded and smiled. He then stood, and left the office.

oOo

Having completed the formalities in the office, Oliver was finally able to take to the streets and start his first patrol.

Dave had chosen to take an unmarked police car out on patrol. It was outfitted with all of the standard equipment, such as blue lights and sirens, but the lights were hidden in the radiator grill and behind the sun visors. He had chosen this vehicle to give Oliver a greater opportunity to spot some traffic offences in order to give him his first taste of dealing with the public.

"Tango-Alpha-seven-one," the police car radio crackled to life. Oliver looked nervously over to his driver, colleague and mentor PC Dave Cox. Dave looked back at him.

"Hey, I ain't gonna answer it, I'm driving," Cox said with a smile on his face. "Just say *Tango-Alpha-seven-one* go ahead, and get ready to write, okay?"

There was a long pause as Oliver composed himself and picked up the handset for the radio. He pressed the *press to talk* (PTT) button on the side of the handset, and cautiously spoke.

"Tango-Alpha-seven-one, go ahead," he said.

Dave gave an approving nod as he listened attentively for the reply from Control.

There was another short pause until the radio crackled into life again. "Tango-Alpha-seven-one, we've had a report of possible rogue trading from a caller who believes their neighbour has been targeted. Can you attend and do a welfare check and see if we've actually got any offences? Are you ready for the address?"

"Go with address," Oliver replied.

Dave listened as the address was given out. It took a moment for him to plot the best route in his head. It was a street he was vaguely familiar with, so there was no need to input it into the car's sat-nav.

As the reported incident was believed to be historic, meaning that it was not happening at that precise moment and that there was no imminent threat or risk, Dave and Oliver attended at *patrol speed,* as they had no lawful authority to exceed the speed limit or contravene any traffic restrictions.

Whilst en-route, Dave instructed Oliver to make contact with Control to request further information about the incident. This had been so far explained to him as being a call in from a neighbour of the person they were going to see. The further information stated that the person they were going to see, a Mr Warby, had previously been targeted by rogue traders and had been conned out of several thousand pounds. The neighbour called police having seen two men attend Mr Warby's address about eight o'clock the previous evening. They were seen to take Mr Warby from his address and drive off, only to bring him back within about thirty minutes.

As Oliver relayed this account to Dave, Dave responded, "Does sound dodgy. There's not a great deal there though, probably best we go and speak to the neighbour first."

It was just after nine a.m. by the time they pulled up outside the home address of the neighbour who had called the police the previous evening. There were no cars on their driveway. It could be that all of the occupants were at work, or it could be that someone was on the school run, or maybe they just didn't drive. Either way, they wouldn't know until they knocked.

From the doorstep they both looked across the road towards Warby's house. The neighbour certainly had a good vantage point from here to see Warby's front door and any activity on the driveway. There was a car sitting on Warby's drive, but it looked like it hadn't been driven in quite some time. Even from across the road the lichen could be seen building up on the windows from moisture that had built up inside the car.

Dave knocked for a second time, still no answer or sign of any activity from within.

"Oh, well, best do what we came here for," he said to Oliver.

They crossed the road and approached Warby's house.

"Wait here a sec," Dave said, "take a moment, tell me what you see."

This question caught Oliver off guard. He knew he was required to respond beyond the obvious, but without experience or aforethought he was temporarily lost for words.

"It's a shit-hole, isn't it," Dave said matter-of-factly. "A place like this is crying out for scumbags to come knocking, asking to do the roof, do the gardening, do the driveway, y'know, the usual shit. And they are very, *very* persuasive. And if this guy's been targeted before, you can guarantee he's on a *sucker's list*."

A sucker's list is a term given to the exchange of information within the criminal fraternity when someone comes across a soft target, a person who is easily susceptible to being manipulated, and has the money to make the effort worthwhile.

Usually, the initial contact is made based on observation, but with an approach, a way in, an introduction. An enquiry about the state of the garden or roof can be a typical introduction. This gets them inside the door, from there it doesn't take long to assess the target for any vulnerabilities, and the likelihood of any concerned and local family members, and more importantly what they're worth. From there, it's just a case of building trust, and playing the waiting game.

"If this guy's been targeted before, it's pretty obvious he and any family haven't learned a bloody thing since then," Dave added.

Oliver surveyed the exterior of the house. It was a sizeable, detached house. But, to quote Dave, it was a 'shit-hole'. The shingled driveway was patchy, Oliver looked back at the road to see so much of it strewn across the pavement. Looking back at the house he saw the front lawn was overgrown. The building itself was in much need of a fresh coat of paint, and the roof had countless broken tiles. He then paused for a moment to consider the value of such a property in this area, £400,000 to £500,000 even in this condition. Amongst all of the houses in the street, *this* would be the one he'd have chosen to call at as a rogue trader, and if he reached that conclusion on his first day on the job, then seasoned fraudsters would undoubtedly reach the same conclusion, time and time again.

They reached the front door. Oliver again began scrutinising it with fresh eyes, eyes that were now open wider than ever before to the ever-increasing evils in society. The paint was flaking on the front door, and the door itself was warped from having absorbed rainwater. The doorbell was missing its casing. Oliver didn't even bother to try it. He knocked, feeling the loose-fitting door reverberate in its frame.

He waited, nothing could be heard from within. He knocked again. Still no reply.

"Call through the letterbox, let them know we're here," Dave suggested.

Oliver crouched down so his face was level with the letterbox, which was about halfway down the door. He poked through to lift the flaps, and pressed his face to the slot.

"Wait!" Dave interrupted before Oliver could say anything. "Not like that. Keep your head to one side of the opening, that way nothing can be poked through at you, okay?"

Oliver took the advice on board and adjusted his position to be to one side of the letterbox. Dave knew there wasn't any likelihood of such violent and antagonistic actions here, but it was a good habit to get the young officer into.

"Also, use your baton to open to flap, *not* your finger, just in case they try to slash at you from the inside, okay?"

From where Oliver was crouched down he looked up at Dave and gave an appreciative nod. He then faced back towards the letterbox. "Police, is there anyone in here?"

When no discernible response came he repeated his call. Still nothing could be heard in reply.

"Okay," Dave said, "well, we're gonna need to get a reply on this. Tell ya what, let's grab a coffee from the petrol station, and we can try again after. The neighbour might be back by then too."

oOo

By the time they had finished their coffees and returned to the address the best part of an hour had passed.

When they pulled up they could see a car parked on the driveway of the neighbour who had originally called the police the previous evening.

"Back to Plan A," Dave said as he parked up, "let's speak to the neighbour first."

"Okay, why's that then?" Oliver asked.

"So, we can get an understanding of why police were called. If you have the luxury of time, which we do now, it's useful to

81

get all the information available before jumping in and speaking to someone who has absolutely no idea that we're even coming. Obviously, if it was an emergency, we would have to jump straight in and play catch-up later. Does that make sense?"

"Absolutely," Oliver replied enthusiastically.

This time when they knocked at the neighbour's house the door was answered. It was answered by a little elderly lady in a baggy sweatshirt and, much to the shock of both Dave and Oliver, skin-tight leggings.

"Mrs Keeble?" Dave asked, "we've come about the call you made to us regarding your neighbour."

"Oh, yes," she replied, "do come in."

Dave beckoned Oliver to follow on behind her, and he brought up the rear, closing the front door behind them. He then went into the living room to find Mrs Keeble and Oliver already sat down. Dave saw the only available seat was next to Oliver as a cat had taken up the only other chair. He chose to remain standing.

Dave continued his opening comment. "We called earlier on, both here and across the road at Mr Warby's. We thought we'd get your take on things first, before speaking to your neighbour. I take it he wouldn't be expecting us?"

"Oh, no, he doesn't know that I've called you," Mrs Keeble said before taking a pause to compose herself and structure her account. "Well, Bernard was targeted by these horrible people about a year ago. They conned him out of many thousands of pounds, he'll never see that money again. It was terrible the effect it had on him. I never really saw him after that, he doesn't go out much at all any more. Before, I used to see him out and about all the time, not now."

"Yes, we are aware of that," Dave interjected, hoping to bring the conversation up to date quicker than Mrs Keeble was allowing it. "What happened last night then, that compelled you to call us?"

"Well, it was last night, it was getting dark, and I was upstairs closing my bedroom curtains. It was then that I saw a van outside Bernard's house, parked right across his driveway, so I thought it must be for him. I thought it strange, for him to have a visitor at that time of night. So, I watched, and I was watching for a good couple of minutes when I saw these two men come out of his house, they came about halfway down the drive and stopped. Then I saw Bernard coming out behind them. They then all got in the van and drove off up the hill."

"Then what happened?" Dave asked.

"Well, I went to finish off a couple of things, but every now and again I looked out of a front window, and after about half an hour I saw the same van pull up again. I saw Bernard get out, and then the van drove off again."

"And which way did the van go?"

"Oh, this time it drove off down the hill," she replied.

"How did Bernard look to you; did he appear upset or in any way distressed?" Dave asked.

"Oh, he just stood at the end of the drive for a few seconds, he looked bewildered. I was about to go out to check on him when he finally went inside. I wasn't dressed for going out, so I thought I'd best call you," Mrs Keeble replied.

"Can you describe the people who were with Bernard when he left his house, and what about the van?" Dave enquired.

"Oh yes, I think so, I'm not sure about the van, all I know is that it was red," Mrs Keeble replied enthusiastically.

Dave then looked across to Oliver who was listening attentively on the sofa. "We're gonna need to grab a quick statement from Mrs Keeble, here," he said throwing the car keys at him, "grab what you need for a statement from the car, may as well get it now."

Oliver caught the keys. He stood up, excused himself and left the room. From where Dave stood he could hear the front door open, but he didn't hear it close.

Dave then stepped out into the hallway to see if Oliver had accidentally left the front door open. He hadn't. Instead, Dave saw Oliver still standing in the hallway, he was peering around the side of the front door. This puzzled Dave. "What are you doing?" he said.

Without averting his gaze, Oliver replied, "There's a red van parked up outside the neighbour's house, I've already got the registration number. I haven't seen anyone with it yet."

Oliver heard Dave's footsteps as he walked back into the living room. He heard his softened voice say, "We've got to go, we'll be back to get the statement later, okay?"

Dave then re-joined Oliver in the hallway. "C'mon then, let's go," he said.

Dave led Oliver across the road, past where he had parked their unmarked police car, and across the far pavement passing the red van, and back up Bernard Warby's driveway.

As before, they knocked. Still there were no sounds coming from within, and certainly no reply. This time they weren't going to be so easily defeated. Dave stepped back from the building and surveyed the frontage up to the roof as he moved along the line of the building towards the side passage between the house and a detached garage. There was a wrought iron gate across the passage, the gate was open.

The gate may very well have been open before, during their earlier visit, but he couldn't recall. He didn't pay it that much attention to it earlier, there was no need to. Dave peered around the corner, along the passage as he ushered Oliver to stay close to the building.

The side passage led between the house and the detached garage. Along it, Dave could see the length of the house and into the garden behind the house. The garage extended beyond the length of the house, as if it continued into a workshop, or what was known as a tandem garage, where two cars can be parked end to end as opposed to the traditional side by side. There were doors that led into the side of the garage extension, one of which was open. Dave could also hear voices.

He then looked back at Oliver and nodded. He then spoke into his radio, "Tango-Alpha-seven-one, possible rogue trading in progress, Fennells Way, suspects still on premises, stand-by."

"All received Tango-Alpha-seven-one," came the reply from control.

Dave quickly briefed Oliver about what was about to happen. He devised a quick plan of action and briefed Oliver as to his part.

"You wait on this corner, okay? This way you can see me in the back garden. From here you can *also* see if anyone comes out of the front door. If they do, give me a shout and challenge them, I'll be round like a shot, okay? From the voices I can hear, and from what happened last night, there's only two of 'em."

Once Oliver had acknowledged his role, Dave cautiously proceeded along the side passage. He came to a halt just before it opened up into the back garden. He was hoping to hear any conversation in greater detail before announcing his arrival.

From the rear corner of the house Dave could see the dilapidated state of the back garden. It was certainly in keeping with the rest of the house. The extension to the garage appeared to be a workshop. The voices had stopped. There was an eerie silence. Dave could feel the adrenaline surging through his body.

He peered around the back of the house. He could now see along its full width. A back door was open. He looked back to check on Oliver before further committing himself into the back garden. Oliver stood in the perfect vantage point, as he had been instructed. He was stood back from the front corner of the house, so he had a clear view down the side passage and also across the front of the house. Dave held his position until Oliver turned to face him. Oliver gave a diver's *okay* hand signal. Dave nodded.

As Dave stepped forward and out of the passage, the line of the building broke visual contact, or what's also known as *line of sight* between him and Oliver. For Oliver this was a particularly tense moment. It was his first day on patrol, and he was effectively left alone to make his own decisions now. Dave was his mentor, but they couldn't be physically attached at all times.

Dave cautiously edged along the rear of the building. He was nearing where the back door was open. He could now hear voices again. He moved closer to the back door. He crouched down, so when he would peer around the door frame he wouldn't be at eye level of anyone who was possibly standing inside. Dave was assuming this room would be the kitchen.

Once low enough Dave peered around the door frame. It was indeed the kitchen, but no one was there. But he could still hear voices, distant voices, deeper within the house. All he could determine was that they were both male, and they were both coming from somewhere inside the house.

Dave repositioned himself out of the sight from the interior of the house and just as he was about to send a radio transmission to advise control and Oliver of the update he was interrupted by

"COPS!" He heard being shouted from somewhere off to his right side.

This made Dave jump and caused him to momentarily lose his balance and fall against the building.

Once composed, and able to turn in the direction of the yell, he saw someone running from the workshop behind the garage towards the far end of the garden.

Dave had a split second to make a decision: should he go after this person, or should he enter the house to determine the welfare of the occupant?

It was a principle that he was familiar with, the welfare of victims supersedes that of detaining suspects. There was an unknown male inside this house with a vulnerable person who was known to live alone.

Dave saw the male disappear over the fence at the end of the garden. He hadn't moved. His attention had again returned to the house by the sound of thunderous footsteps coming down the stairs.

Dave again stood up, and he was in the process of entering the kitchen when he could see the front door being flung wide open and a figure disappearing into the stark brightness beyond the dimly lit hallway.

Dave then made his way along the hallway as quickly as he could, giving a momentary glance up the stairs as he passed them, before disappearing out of the front door. It was then he could hear shouting coming from outside.

"Get off me, get off me."

Once outside he had to give himself a moment for his eyes to readjust to the brightness of the morning sky, the sun was still low and beaming directly at him.

It was then he could hear the same voice continuing his protests. "Get the fuck off me, man, what the fuck are you doing?"

Dave then saw that Oliver had restrained this man on the driveway. He had him face down with one arm behind his back in a half-Nelson position.

He then went over to help Oliver handcuff him by bringing his other arm behind his back to meet the first. Once cuffed, Dave asked, "Have you said the magic words?"

A puzzled look came over Oliver's face, *magic words*, he thought.

"Have you nicked him?" Dave said in simpler terms.

"Um, no, not yet," Oliver replied whilst trying to catch his breath.

"Better say 'em now then," said Dave.

"I am arresting you on suspicion of…" Oliver faltered, he looked up at Dave for guidance.

"Let's go with *fraud by false representation*," Dave suggested."

"…fraud by false representation," Oliver concluded. He then expertly recited the caution, as well as advising the man that he was being arrested *to ensure a prompt and effective investigation of the alleged offence.*

They then both helped the man get to his feet. Whilst Oliver maintained control of him, Dave took a step back. It was then that he saw the man had sustained a deep cut across the bridge of his nose as well as the cuts to his knuckles that he had noticed when he was cuffing him.

"What happened, did you trip running out of the front door?" Dave asked the man.

"Your boy did it, went fucking schizo on me he did, you wanna keep that one on a short leash," the man replied.

Dave looked over at Oliver who had a *butter wouldn't melt in his mouth* type look on his face.

The man started frantically looking around.

"If you're looking for your buddy, he's left you high and dry, my friend," Dave said. He then continued to say to Oliver, "Why don't you quickly pop inside to check on the old boy, make it a quick in and out, tell him we'll have someone come back to see him and get a statement? I'll be okay here."

Oliver extended his arms to allow Dave to get a hold of the man. He then left the two of them standing on the driveway and approached the open front door. Before entering, he glanced back to see that neither Dave or the man had moved.

Oliver stepped inside the front door, again having to give his eyes a moment to adjust. "Mister Warby, it's the police, are you okay?"

No reply came, Oliver repeated himself, "Mister Warby, it's the police."

Oliver didn't know the man he had arrested had come from upstairs. So, Oliver felt it logical to search the house for Mr Warby finishing off downstairs before starting a new floor. From where he stood he could see all the way through into the galley kitchen at the far end of the hallway. So, to clear the floor all he need do was stick his head around the corner into the living room to check that room was all in order.

Oliver peered around the living room door, "Mister Warby," he called.

With the ground floor now cleared, he went back to the foot of the stairs. He tilted himself to get a glimpse of Dave outside, to check he was still okay, before venturing upstairs.

"Mister Warby," he called as he ascended the stairs, "it's the police."

The first door off the landing was the bathroom, then a bedroom, these rooms would be to the rear of the property. Then came what Oliver expected to be the main bedroom. He entered.

As he stepped into the room, where it opened up beyond the door, he saw an elderly man, sitting on his bed looking down towards his feet. His coat was strewn at his feet. He appeared to be clutching what Oliver initially thought to be a passport, but turned out to be a building society book. Oliver maintained his distance, so as not to startle him.

"Mister Warby," he asked in a much softer voice.

After a delay of a couple of seconds, the seated man's head slowly elevated until he was looking eye to eye with Oliver. It could clearly be seen that he had recently been crying.

Oliver approached him, and taking precautions not to step on his coat, he crouched down in front of him.

"Mister Warby, sir, are you okay?" Oliver asked.

He could see Mr Warby still clutching what he could now clearly see to be a building society book as if his life depended on it. His hands were strong, but his fingers were long and thin, his skin was brown, and covered with liver spots. As Oliver looked at his hands, a single tear landed on the back of one and flowed away into nothingness.

Oliver wanted to stay with Mr Warby, but he remembered what Dave had told him.

"Mister Warby, are you going to be okay, sir? I've got to go now, the man who was here has been arrested. We're gonna have someone pop in shortly to get a statement from you, is that okay?"

There was nothing in the way of a response from Mr Warby; Oliver was unsure if anything he had just said had been understood, or even heard.

"Mister Warby, will you be okay?" Oliver paused, he witnessed Mr Warby give only the faintest of nods.

"Would you like me to ask your neighbour to pop over, she was looking out for you, that's why we're here?" Oliver asked.

The nod continued. "Okay," said Oliver, "we'll ask her to pop over, and we'll have someone come to see you shortly."

With that Oliver stood up and stepped back. He then walked back towards the door. He turned to have one last glance of Mr Warby, seeing him in exactly the same position, his head had again dropped.

Once outside again, Oliver had a momentary moment of panic as Dave and the arrested man weren't where he had left them. He hurriedly walked down the driveway, giving a passing glance along the side passage. But at that moment, to his relief Dave came into view, propped up against their unmarked police car as it came into view beyond the arrested man's van.

"What took you so long?" Dave enquired as Oliver re-joined him on the pavement.

"He was *very* upset," Oliver replied.

"Yeah, I'm not surprised, it's a despicable thing to do to old folk," Dave said with an increasing volume with the sole intention of having the arrested man hear him from his new place in the back of the car.

"Oliver," Dave started, "meet Mister Ryan Keenan," indicating to the man sat before him. Oliver stooped down so he could look in to see the prisoner handcuffed on the back seat.

In the time he had been inside, Dave had repositioned the handcuffs so that Keenan now sat with his arms loosely folded and rested in his lap. He was cuffed in such a way that he was no longer able to straighten his arms, thus preventing him from lashing out at anyone.

Dave looked over the top of Oliver as he peered in. "Are you cold in there, Ryan?" he asked.

Keenan continued to look straight ahead, he merely shrugged his shoulders in response to the question asked of him.

"Perhaps nervous then, I mean you're sat there trembling like a shitting dog," Dave concluded.

Trembling like a shitting dog, this immediately conjured up a barrage of imagery for Oliver. All of a sudden, all Oliver could visualise was a Jack Russell or Chihuahua engaged in a full body convulsion trying to take care of business. He had to move out of any view that Keenan might have of him before letting out a raucous laugh. He had never heard that expression before, but it was one he'd be sure to remember. Once Oliver had composed himself, he quickly popped over to ask the neighbour to check in on Mr Warby before he joined Keenan in the back seat. Dave had already retaken his position behind the wheel.

From there, Dave and Oliver took Keenen to the local custody suite. Oliver wasn't able to sit up front as he had before. He was now responsible for his prisoner, and as a result had to sit alongside him throughout the journey to custody. As they were transporting Keenan in a car, Oliver had the added responsibility of protecting the driver should Keenan misbehave along the way.

Having arrived in custody, and after Keenan was booked in, in addition to completing the required paperwork, Oliver was required to do an extra form, called a *Use of Force* form, for the physical restraint he had used to secure Keenan prior to Dave coming out of the house. Dave was unsure what techniques or tactics had been used, and his account on this form would state that. But, he concluded, for Oliver to subdue a significantly larger man, desperate to get away in such an efficient way, albeit it with injuries, however minor, whatever he did, it was effective.

"Some of the things you'll witness in this job will be fucking awful, the trick is not to let them get to you, and certainly try *not* to take them home with you. You did good today."

These were Dave's parting words at the end of Oliver's first day on the job.

Chapter Ten

The next day was also an early shift for Oliver. His team and department worked a ten-day rotation. This consisted of two early shifts, of which this was the second, to be followed by two late shifts, which started at three p.m. and finished at midnight. Then finally, two night-shifts, which start at ten p.m. and finished at seven a.m. the following morning. This was then followed by four rest days, before the rotation started over.

During the briefing, the officers were given their call-signs for the shift. Oliver and Dave were again TA71, *Tango-Alpha-seven-one*. The Sergeant also gave out specific work assignments to some officers. As TA71 was a double-crewed unit, a unit consisting of two officers, they were assigned to attempt the arrest of the person believed to be the outstanding suspect for their rogue trading job. This was the man who had run from Dave in the back garden of the house they had attended the previous day.

Had it not fallen this way – to have Dave and Oliver make the attempt – it would have made sense to send them along anyway, as Dave should readily be able to identify the man based on their previous encounter.

The name of the man they were after was provided during the interview with the man who Oliver arrested; Ryan Keenan. Evidently, Keenan gave up his accomplice in an attempt to curry favour by co-operating. The name of the man they were looking to arrest was Wayne Corbett.

"No honour among thieves," said Dave to Oliver as they were handed the assignment. Oliver just smiled. Although he was nineteen, he was still naïve about certain things, and this wasn't a phrase he was familiar with. His dad had always taught him that if you don't understand something to never be ashamed to seek clarification, either that or remain silent, instead of blurting out anything nonsensical as a reply. On this occasion, Oliver felt it prudent to simply remain silent.

By the time they had readied their vehicle for the shift it was just after seven thirty a.m. Dave had deliberately chosen to use an unmarked police car again, but not the same one as the day before. The reason for this was so they could park near to their suspect's home address without drawing too much attention to themselves. Also, should they knock on the door and someone peeked out of a window first, they may choose not to answer the door knowing it was the police.

Unfortunately, under legislation, the police must have a firm belief that an offender is on the premises to be able to force entry. Just calling at someone's home address does not fulfil this requirement. Using the unmarked car was not infallible, but it may improve their odds slightly.

After the work they did the previous shift, this would be a relatively easy assignment. As a result of the Keenan arrest, all of the necessary evidence would have been obtained. In this instance it would include statements from both the victim, Bernard Warby, and his neighbour whose suspicions involved the police in the first place. Also, depending on the CID investigation, financial evidence may have also been requested. This may take the form of bank statements in order to prove that cash withdrawals had been made as well as any other transactions. However, as this was not specified within their assignment, all Oliver and Dave would be required to do is attend the address, and should the suspect, Wayne Corbett, be there, then he was to be arrested for the same offence as Keenan had been, Fraud by False Representation.

This offence covers a multitude of sins, it can involve a suspect pretending to be someone they're not or, as in this case, taking money for work that either didn't need to be carried out, or wasn't carried out at all.

By the time Dave and Oliver pulled into Dudley Crescent they had all the information they needed. Corbett, like Keenan, was a prolific offender, they were known accomplices, having been linked on many of each other's offences over the years. Also, they both had a string of previous convictions for similar offences, where they had targeted the elderly and vulnerable, had claimed work needed to be done, then took money both before and after the work had apparently been completed. So, it wouldn't have taken much longer to be knocking on Corbett's door had Keenan not decided to drop his name. Maybe this had factored into his decision, giving the police information, they could easily obtain by other means holds no value.

According to the local police database, both were also sought in connection with numerous other offences which matched their MO, or *Modus Operandi*. This is essentially a typical method under which they operate, potentially involving a tried and tested plan that has previously achieved a positive result for them which they have stuck to, and has become habitual over time. As a result, this method has been identified as being theirs, so when an incident is reported in which a similar method has been adopted, then Keenan and Corbett need to be spoken to regarding any knowledge they may have.

The previous day would have been an ideal opportunity to speak to them both, because their involvement in the Warby incident would be indisputable. Then when questioned about similar offences they may admit to them. Also, they would be given the opportunity to admit to any offences not put to them in order to give them the opportunity for a clean sheet. These are known as TIC offences, *Taken Into Consideration.*

Dave parked the unmarked police car a couple of doors down from Corbett's house. They didn't put their police flat hats on, and they wore their black overcoats, which were thigh length waterproof coats which had a Police sign on them, but in such a way that it could be folded back on itself and concealed under a Velcro flap. This was how it was worn today.

It was still early as they approached the front door. They had discussed en-route how they were going to play it, but the final decisions weren't able to be made until they had reached the house. With this information now available to them Dave was able to finalise the plan.

"Okay, this time I'll stay around front and knock, you go around the side and keep an eye out in case he goes out the back. He's a runner, we know that from yesterday," he said.

Dave stood close to the building until Oliver was in position.

When all was ready Dave knocked, *we should have a second unit for this,* he thought.

Dave was right, they should have a second unit, at the very least one more officer. He had made the request after briefing, but because they had less than the minimum number of officers working that day due to leave, sickness, and training, one car was all the Sergeant could assign. Although they were double-crewed, in essence they weren't two independent officers as Oliver was being mentored and shouldn't ideally be left on his own. But Dave was trying to achieve the best he could with the resources he had. He could keep them both together on the doorstep, but should Corbett go running out of the back, like so many do, then the odds of catching up with him would be zero. The previous day's exploits showed how nimble Corbett was on his feet when he so chose to be.

Again, the previous day had proved Oliver's abilities to Dave, and as a result he felt confident in him. He had a wisdom and a maturity beyond his years, a quiet confidence, despite his naivety. Dave liked him, and wasn't going to put him in any situation he didn't feel he could handle.

After the knock, Dave could hear movement from inside the house. Then, within a few seconds the front door opened. A middle-aged woman stood there in the open doorway. She stood there for the eight a.m. world to see, dressed in a pink dressing gown, which barely covered not nearly as much as it should.

Not many reflective surfaces in this house, Dave thought.

She didn't say a word, certainly not a greeting, or the half expected, "What the fuck do you want?" which is a typical response to getting a Copper on the doorstep before breakfast.

"Morning, is Wayne home?" Dave casually asked.

"Yeah, he's here, what the fuck's he done now?" came the reply.

"Now you know I can't tell ya that," Dave replied.

As if by magic, or because he had been listening to the conversation thus far, a figure started stomping down the stairs. At first, all that could be seen were feet, then feet and legs dressed in blue and white striped pyjama trousers, rather disconcertingly with a hand down the front of them.

Note to self, do not shake hands, Dave thought.

Then the figure emerged full length. Dave instantly recognised him to be the same man he saw all too briefly the previous day.

"Hello again," Dave said with more than a hint of sarcasm.

The greeting was wasted on Corbett, who was either ignoring the remark having understood it, or was not fully awake yet and it went completely over his head.

"We kinda met yesterday, albeit briefly," Dave continued, "can I come in?"

"Why? What's this about?" Corbett asked.

"I need to have a little chat with you, now I can do this on the doorstep with you with your hand down your pants, or we can do it inside where the hand down your pants is optional," Dave said, the sarcasm evidently building in his tone.

"All right, all right," Corbett said as he nodded his head to one side to indicate to Dave to come in. He then turned to the woman. "You got a fag?"

They both turned and led the way for Dave to follow them down the hallway. He pushed the front door to, but didn't close it, so Oliver would have a way in.

As Dave entered the kitchen at the end of the hallway he saw Oliver standing menacingly and prominently in the middle of the Corbett's back garden. He then placed his hand on his radio to call control to have Oliver join him inside.

Dave thought for a moment that if Corbett had given consideration to run, the mere sight of Oliver's menacing presence stood in his way would most likely have made him think twice. Dave walked past where the woman was lighting a cigarette for Corbett. He rapped his knuckle against the kitchen window until he got Oliver's attention, and then signalled him to join him inside.

After a few seconds Oliver joined them indoors. The kitchen wasn't large enough to comfortably accommodate them all, so he remained in the hallway.

As a mentor, it was Dave's responsibility to prepare Oliver for independent patrol, making him proficient in his decision making as much as in policy and procedure. Much of that could be taught to him, but equally as much would be by him making his own decisions, but with Dave there as a safety net.

Dave then said to Corbett. "Listen to what my colleague has to say."

This was a rehearsed prompt for Oliver to then arrest Corbett on the same grounds as which Keenan had been arrested on the previous day.

Corbett was then escorted upstairs by Dave in order for him to get more appropriately dressed for leaving the house.

As Dave passed Oliver to go upstairs, he asked of him, "Can you call up and say we've got one in custody and have them make CID aware?"

A few minutes later, Dave came back down, he walked a couple of steps behind a more appropriately dressed Corbett.

Oliver then led them all outside to where their car was parked. He held the rear nearside passenger door open for Corbett to get in. After closing the door, Dave said to him, "Whatever you do, don't shake his hand."

Again, as with the *honour amongst thieves* comment, this was in essence wasted on Oliver, but he would abide by it, hoping for an explanation later.

It was protocol for a prisoner, someone who was in custody, to sit in the rear nearside, kerbside passenger seat. The reason for this is to put them at the furthest distance from the driver. The second officer, in this case Oliver, would sit behind the driver, next to the prisoner. His role is to monitor the prisoner and to intervene as necessary in order to protect the driver. However, should the risk be such that this is anticipated then either the prisoner should be handcuffed, or they should be transported in a van with a purpose-built cell in the rear.

Given Corbett's previous offending history, a lack of violence warnings, and his physical stature, Dave felt it adequate to make the short drive to custody in the car without the need to handcuff him.

He did, however, give Corbett a warning. "Right, we're not gonna cuff you, but if you choose to play silly buggers and I have to pull over, then you *will* be getting cuffed, do you understand me?"

The journey to custody was uneventful, and Corbett was indeed well behaved. He was booked in without any incident under the same report reference that Keenan's arrest had already created.

Once they left custody, Dave had to update the incident report and Oliver had to complete a statement detailing the arrest. The last line of his statement read;

I left custody at 0912 hrs having no further dealings with this prisoner.

Chapter Eleven

A couple of weeks later, Oliver found he had been tasked to view an update on the report regarding his arrests of Keenan and Corbett. Once he followed the link in an email he saw that the investigation had been discontinued, and that Keenan and Corbett, who had been released under investigation following their arrests and initial interviews, had been advised that *No Further Action* would be taken against either of them with regards to the matter involving Bernard Warby.

It was also explained that the decision was made because Keenan had been arrested the next day. The day after he and Corbett had taken Warby from his home address to get the cash from the ATM. This hadn't allowed time for any fraud to take place.

It was admitted that they did take Warby from his home to a local ATM cash machine, but that only persuasion, not coercion was used. Only £200 had been handed over, for which a receipt was issued for gardening work to be done, and that the £200 was for items to be purchased to carry out said work.

At the time Keenan, and in turn, Corbett, was arrested no fraud had in fact taken place, as they hadn't been given the opportunity to defraud Warby.

They both went *no comment* in interview, so nothing was gained from that, except for the possibility of an inference being drawn should the case ever go as far as Court. However, it was agreed that the £200 be returned to Mr Warby, and that neither suspect should attend his address again to seek work.

So, what was left wasn't much, and when a charging decision was sought from a Prosecuting Barrister it was deemed that there wasn't a likely chance of conviction, and as a result, the case was dropped.

"For fuck's sake," Oliver exclaimed.

"What's up?" Dave said scooting his office chair around the end of the desk in order to see Oliver's screen.

"Those two scumbags have been let off for ripping off that old boy," Oliver said with disgust.

"Yeah, it happens, better get used to it," Dave replied, "did they say why?"

"They went no comment in interview," Oliver replied, thinking that was the question asked.

"No, no, why was the case dropped?" Dave emphasised.

"Oh, um, coz we nicked 'em the next day, we didn't give them a chance to commit the fraud," Oliver explained.

"Well, some things can't be helped, unfortunate circumstances, we couldn't very well turn up at the neighbours and then walk away from the old boy knowing they were there, much like we couldn't *not* arrest them having found them there. There's no two ways to deal with this, we did all we could. Sometimes it goes this way," Dave said in an attempt to console the obviously upset and angered Oliver.

"I saw his face though, Warby, he'll be devastated when he's told," Oliver said.

"They won't send it to Court without evidence, and by the sounds of it there wasn't any. You can't just punish people without the evidence. It's a shit situation I know, shame it's your first, but you'll get used to it, roll on to the next one," Dave paused, "how else would you have done this?"

Dave thought this had all fallen on deaf ears, because there was absolutely no reaction whatsoever from Oliver.

Chapter Twelve

Later in that same block of shifts, Oliver and Dave were on mobile patrol. They had found a break in their assigned workload and felt like getting out of the office.

This, for them was a late shift, working from three p.m. until midnight. The night shift had come in at ten p.m., so they were taking the calls that were coming in. Oliver and Dave kept their call-sign, but they weren't being deployed to any calls.

Apart from being an excuse to get out of the office for a while, it was useful for Dave to be able to show Oliver the area they covered from their station. As well as possibly getting in some 'vehicle stops' to give Oliver further practice at engaging the public.

They weren't far from the station, certainly nowhere near the boundary of their ground. They were patrolling a residential estate that had been brought up in briefing for anti-social behaviour (ASB) in the form of youths on scooters. There had been numerous reports recently of a group, always believed to be the same youths, seen tearing around the streets, pulling wheelies and generally being a nuisance.

"Dunno what we're s'posed to do if we actually see the little fuckers," Dave said having mentioned to Oliver that this was the area they were terrorising.

"There's still nothing in black and white to say we can chase 'em or do *anything*. So, it'll be sightings only, okay. I ain't risking my pension for one of these little twats!"

Oliver just sat back in his seat, smiled, and nodded along. He had some thoughts in his head as to what he would like to do. One of the thoughts that occurred to him was the use the HolSTyDS equipment in the boot. HolSTyDS stands for *Hollow Spike Tyre Deflation System,* or a *Stinger* as it is more commonly known. To the uninitiated, this is an approximately twenty-five-foot (when open and in use) strip of sharply pointed hollow metal spikes arranged on a collapsible frame for storage.

The idea is to be in the path of a fleeing subject vehicle, and whilst taking cover from behind a solid barrier to either throw out, or drag the Stinger strip across the road in front of the vehicle, but, and there is a but, being able to withdraw it from the road before any pursuing vehicles also drive over it. The pursuing vehicles will be aware of the Stinger deployment and deliberately hold back to give the officer more time, but not that much more.

Once the subject vehicle has driven over the Stinger, the hollow spikes would puncture the tyres and allow a gradual deflation. This was intended to allow the car to gradually become more difficult to control and force the occupants to abandon the pursuit. It does not have the intention of bursting the tyres as Hollywood would have us believe.

However, Stinger deployment had not been approved for motorcycle or scooter pursuits, due to the high risk to the rider, and invariably a pillion passenger.

But this wasn't swaying Oliver from conjuring up a scenario in his head, and putting the training he had received on the Stinger to very good use.

It was certainly more efficient, and civilised than the alternative he had come up with. He doubted he would find tying a length of piano wire between two lampposts would be found anywhere in the Manuals of Policing.

When in town, windows down, went through Oliver's head as they drove through the estate. This was a little catch-phrase taught to him on his basic driving course. It essentially means that when in a built-up area, have the windows down so you can hear what's going on around you. In this case, they both had their windows down, and they could hear the high-pitched screech of either scooters or someone's two-stroke lawnmower. The noises were on the move, and neither of them was able to determine if in fact they were getting closer at all.

As they progressed along the main road of the estate Dave indicated off towards a side road. "That's where he lives." As if expecting Oliver to be psychic in his abilities and know exactly who he was talking about.

"Who?" Came Oliver's tentative reply, feeling as if he had missed something preceding the remark.

"Keenan," Dave said, "he lives down the end there, on the right."

At that, Dave braked to a halt and put the car into reverse. He then backed up far enough to make the turn into the road. "Let's go see if he's home," Dave said.

From the outset of this shift Dave had to settle for a marked police car, one with the blue and yellow Battenberg markings and a roof bar of blue and red lights. But he was able to get his hands on his preferred unmarked car after his colleagues had handed their vehicles over to the night shift. This one was a black Ford Focus hatchback, nothing sporty, but it was inconspicuous.

As they turned into the side street they could see that the local council had adopted the energy saving policy of only illuminating every other streetlamp. It was either that, or they were in need of quite a few repairs.

The road was wide enough to turn a car in, with a single side of parking, or where there was a gap in the double parking. But this wasn't to be the case today. Dave knew of a bank of en-block garages beyond the houses, so he maintained his speed along the length of the road and turned the car around within the garages. He then parked up in the shadows of the garages and turned the engine off.

"That's his place, y'see it? First one on the left," Dave said.

"I see it," Oliver said as he nodded.

"That's probably his truck in front too, I'll run it through," Dave said referring to the white crew-cab tipper truck parked directly in front of Keenan's house.

Running it through meant utilising the police's access to the registration databases of the DVLA. After a moment Dave had the result of the checks.

"Hmmm, it's coming back as previous keeper details only, no insurance details held either. Chances are it's his, and he's up to his old tricks in it. Y'see, it's parked facing outwards, probably for a quick getaway," Dave reported.

Previous keeper details only meant that the new, or current owner of the vehicle had yet to advise the DVLA of the transfer of ownership. Which meant the DVLA and police had no means of tracking the driver or owner in the event of any incident. This is an offence in itself. The fact that the van didn't have any insurance was not an immediate cause for concern as quite often a driver can drive a vehicle on a Driver Policy, or on insurance held for another vehicle which allows the policyholder to drive other vehicles.

They watched, and they waited.

"Are we actually expecting something to happen whilst we're sat here?" Oliver asked.

"Nah, not really," Dave replied, "but it beats doing stuff."

Oliver chuckled. He then remembered back to his training. "Don't we need one of those *ripper* things for this kinda thing?"

"Of course not," Dave replied. "You're just sat in a car, I'm about to have a fag. Just coz I chose to park in the dark, is so they can't see me having this fag, and has absolutely nothing to do with Keenan," Dave laughed.

The *ripper* to which Oliver eluded was in fact a RIPA, or Regulations of Investigatory Powers Act, which governs and regulates certain covert police powers and procedures. Had they been targeting Keenan, or anyone in particular, and been covert in doing so, then they would need to explain their actions and their reasons for doing so. But Dave was right, they were merely sat in an unmarked police car, in uniform in plain sight, apart from the fact that the street was dimly lit.

Just as Dave had finished rolling his fag and placed his hand on the interior handle of his door, he paused. Ahead of them, walking towards them was a silhouette. It was lost intermittently due to the spacing between the streetlamps. But it was a silhouette of a man, and whoever it was, he was getting closer.

Then there was a trip, and a stumble, then a lot of cursing as if someone else was to blame. They both deduced that this man was a little worse for wear. Most likely having just walked back from the pub just around the corner.

Despite his aforementioned affliction, he was actually steering a steady course down the middle of the road. As he got closer, level with the last houses, they could both make out sufficient features and characteristics to recognise the man to be Keenan. He showed no sign of turning towards his house. For a moment both Dave and Oliver felt that Keenan may continue beyond his house and on towards the garages where they were parked. In unison, they slouched down in their seats to disappear below the level of the dashboard.

Keenan continued towards their unmarked police Ford Focus. He appeared to be on the tail end of a long drinking session. He kept coming, ever closer, and Dave and Oliver sank even lower in their seats.

Then Keenan stopped. He was level with the front of their car. He turned to face away from it and dropped his weight down on the nearside wing. The suspension collapsed under his added weight. He was blissfully unaware that he was being watched.

Both Dave and Oliver started sniggering like a couple of schoolgirls. At one point it was Dave, the older, more sensible and mature of the two of them, who had to cup his hands over his mouth to stifle his laughter. Oliver proved somewhat more adept at composing himself.

They watched Keenan, their eyes peeked over the top edge of the dashboard. They were enveloped in darkness. Even had Keenan looked directly at them, he wouldn't see any outlines.

Then in a moment, Keenan spun around to face the car. He slapped both hands down on the bonnet. He was bent over at the waist, so his torso was horizontal. He was supported by his outstretched arms which rested on the car. He started retching.

"He's gonna puke," Dave whispered.

Within a second, the first delivery took flight.

"Oh, no," Dave said, "not all over my fucking car."

In an instant the tables were turned. It started off with Dave and Oliver having fun at Keenan's expense. But now it was Keenan who would certainly be having the last laugh.

"Y'know what," Dave began, "we should do him right now! No one would know."

Not for the first time that evening their thoughts were in unison. This echoed the thoughts racing through Oliver's mind. For a moment Oliver began to open his mouth, to actually verbalise a response, to confirm to his colleague and mentor what a good idea that actually was, and that they should enact it, now!

Oliver's mouth was open, ready to speak, but for some reason the words never followed. Why not? They had agreed on this course of action. He knew what he wanted to say, but he also knew he shouldn't say it. He did want to pummel Keenan, but did Dave? How could he be sure? He couldn't, and until he could, he needed to remain quiet.

Although Oliver remained silent, the air around the car was far from quiet, as Keenan sent a second and third airmail shipment after the first. Then there was silence. They could both see heavy breathing from Keenan, his whole torso was rising and falling. He remained supported by the pebble-dashed Focus for a couple of minutes.

Eventually, Keenan stood upright. He staggered for a moment, having to rely on the car again to centre his balance. He was directly facing where Oliver sat. Oliver had the advantage of Keenan not knowing he was there. But also, not being inebriated. It wouldn't have been a fair fight.

Fair? What does scum like this know about fair, Oliver thought. Ripping off an old boy of his life savings isn't fair.

Oliver was again grateful for the darkness the interior of the car afforded him. He felt confident there was no way that Dave would see the look of gritted hated on his face, and his fists tightly clenched. Unbeknown to Oliver, his hand was actually reaching for the interior door handle. Once he realised this, he cautiously withdrew it.

Keenan had finally composed himself. He was again confident in his abilities to stand unassisted, so much so that he took his hands from the side of the car. He tested his balance for a moment, before slowly turning around to face towards his destination, his front door. Now, with his sights set on his new target, he set off.

Keenan was so pre-occupied with the door that his sights were too high to see any obstacles before him. He tripped as he went up the kerb, much to Dave and Oliver's renewed amusement, then also negotiating the front lawn, walking corner to corner proved problematic. Before finally trying to make a key fit in a keyhole.

Dave and Oliver began to grow impatient at the time this had started to take. They couldn't move off with Keenan still standing in the street. They needed to ensure he was out of sight before starting the engine. Eventually, the key was made to fit the keyhole. The door opened, much to Keenan's apparent surprise as it was until then holding him up much as the car had done for him earlier. Then the door closed as upstairs lights turned on.

"Fucking hell," Dave exclaimed, "we'd better fuck off before there's a fucking domestic here."

With that Dave started the car, and he drove half the length of the street, far beyond where Keenan could see, before turning the headlights on.

"I ain't taking this back to the nick like this," he said. "Nah, fuck that, I'd sooner pay a fiver down at the BP to get it washed. I ain't touching his puke."

After the car was washed and filled up with fuel, Dave finally got to enjoy his cigarette in the loading area behind the petrol station building.

"Don't say a word of this to anyone, okay," he said to Oliver.

"Not a word, we were *never* there," Oliver replied as he drew pinched fingers across his lips.

Chapter Thirteen

After his last night shift, Oliver got home from work at about seven thirty a.m. As he walked through the front door he was first greeted by the smell of fresh coffee and bacon before his father set eyes on him and welcomed him home. "Good shift?" his father asked.

Oliver nodded his response amidst a yawn which he was delayed in catching. His father gave him a disapproving look. A look that Oliver had been on the receiving end of many times during his life. To Oliver, it was a look that said, 'I brought you up with better manners than that'. Oliver mouthed the word "sorry" as he continued into the kitchen. He dropped his rucksack on the floor and pulled out a stool at the breakfast bar and sat himself down.

"Do you want anything of anything before you go to sleep?" his father asked whilst in the process of pouring himself a coffee.

Oliver knew a coffee wouldn't be the best thing to have right now, and seeing the bacon sandwich that his father had made for himself had put him off the idea of that too.

"Nah, I think I'm just gonna crash," Oliver replied.

"Okay," his father replied, "are you around this evening? Would be nice to have some time together."

This was a stark realisation for them both. It was true, in the time that Oliver had been out of training school and working his shift pattern, he had hardly spent any time with his father, and when they were both at home at the same time either one, or the other was distracted or resting. If Oliver was home during the day because of his rotation his father was invariably working, or Oliver was too tired to be able to be sociable.

"Sounds good," Oliver said as he stood, now towering over his father who had taken a stool next to his. Oliver leant over and kissed his father on the top of his head before snatching up his rucksack from the floor and heading towards the stairs.

"Night," his father called up behind him.

No reply came, his father put it down to Oliver being out of range to hear him.

A little tit-bit of information that Dave had bestowed upon Oliver was how to best cope with working the shift pattern they did. The rotation they worked consisted of two early shifts, followed by two late shifts working until midnight, then two night shifts, followed by four days off. Dave had worked this pattern for many years, and had refined a system for readjusting to the days off which worked well for him.

Dave had found that staying up late after the second late shift better prepared the body for the transition onto night shifts. He had a habit of staying up until three or four in the morning before turning in. This way he would be compelled to sleep into the afternoon, and be better rested by the time he went to work at ten p.m. He had tried getting up as normal in the morning and having a nap in the afternoon or evening before the night shift, but this was rarely successful. He found that forcing your body to sleep when it doesn't want, or need to is futile.

Dave also found that the best way to readjust the body clock to being awake during the day after the last night shift, and thus gaining maximum benefit of their days off, was to only allow himself to sleep until midday, maybe one o'clock after finishing at seven a.m. This way he was able to gain some benefit and productivity from that day, and not be sleeping through one of his days off. But more importantly, he would be going through the day on minimal sleep. Which would mean he would be exhausted by the end of the day, having the benefit of sleeping better that first night *and* be fully adjusted to being awake during the day by the following morning. Again, by trial and error, Dave had found that if he had allowed himself to sleep too long after coming off the last night shift, then he would be too rested that night, and his body would be ready thinking it had another shift to go, resulting in him being unable to sleep. Others had the habit of pushing through, and not going to bed after the night shift until that evening. Dave tried it, and gave up on it because it left him feeling like a zombie and the day wasn't in any way productive.

So far, Oliver found Dave's suggestion to be working. He didn't like the idea of setting an alarm within five hours of going to bed, but he knew he would make best use of the rest of the first day off, and he would sleep well that night.

oOo

However, Dave wasn't quite so aware of the other favour he did Oliver, that night when they washed Keenan's puke off their car.

Now Oliver knew Keenan's address, what vehicle he drove, and possibly where he liked to have a drink of an evening, and that he would most likely walk home afterwards on his own. He knew all this without having to draw any attention to himself at work by accessing police records.

With this information to hand, it allowed Oliver to entertain thoughts that probably wouldn't have occurred to him. Since washing the puke off their car, Oliver was waiting for an opportunity to revisit his street and take a closer look, and to familiarise himself with the area a little bit.

Oliver didn't know if it was a good thing or a bad thing that his night shifts were uneventful. Being sat quietly beside Dave wasn't anything unusual, but his mind was allowed to work overtime as it wasn't being kept busy. He kept seeing the tearful look on the face of Bernard Warby, and the smug look of arrogance and defiance on the face of Keenan in custody, knowing he would beat this rap and avoid being charged, as he had on so many occasions in the past.

Whilst the investigation was still ongoing, prior to the decision to drop it, Dave showed Oliver numerous reports of a similar nature that had possible links to Keenan. These were filed for various reasons; insufficient evidence to bring a charge, unreliable victim or witnesses, or in the case of Oliver's arrest, it had been deemed that no crime had actually taken place.

Either way, the more Oliver thought about it, the more it enraged him. He was undecided how he felt about how Mr Warby was informed that the case had been dropped. Was he glad that he didn't have to do it personally, or did he feel like he was short-changing the pensioner-veteran who had spent a lifetime serving and protecting his country, only to be let down in his moment of desperation and need? But beneath the confusion, was an underlying and unwavering feeling that was bubbling to the surface.

oOo

Although Oliver had set an alarm for midday, he was well awake in time to hear it go off. He got dressed and went downstairs.

There he saw the remnants of his father's breakfast on the side. There was a half-eaten bacon sandwich, drowning in brown sauce, and the dregs of a cup of coffee next to it. On the cooker hob was a frying pan. More rashers were lying in the pan. Oliver deduced that his father had intentionally cooked too much for his own breakfast, in the hope that Oliver would join him.

He went to the fridge and took a couple of slices from a loaf of bread. Then he reheated the bacon from the pan in the microwave, before adding them to the unbuttered bread, plus a sensible amount of brown sauce to make his breakfast. That, along with a glass of orange juice would be enough to tide him over.

Oliver then spent a few minutes tidying the kitchen so that his father wouldn't have to do it upon his return from work. He then headed out.

Outside, Oliver looked at his car sitting on the driveway. He remotely unlocked it, approached it, but he paused as he took hold of the door handle. He looked around. He then turned and walked away from his car, locking it as he went, and walked off down the street.

Oliver had an idea of what today was going to entail. With that in mind, and coupled with the pleasant weather, he felt that it would probably be best to take the bus.

A perk of being a police officer that Oliver had been made aware of was free bus travel within the Force county. All Oliver had to do was present his ID card to the driver and he would be allowed to travel for free anywhere in the county. The only downside would be that if an incident took place on the bus then the driver would expect Oliver to take charge of the situation. When he was informed about this perk, Oliver was told that it was advisable to never use it whilst he was drunk. This is because, should anything take place, and he was required to get involved he would effectively be putting himself on duty whilst in an intoxicated state, and would effectively be drunk on duty, which is a disciplinary offence. Oliver didn't have an issue with this.

Oliver took a single bus for the majority of his intended journey and walked the remainder of the route to where he needed to be. He could've got a connecting bus and avoided the necessity to walk, but it was a pleasant enough day and he wanted to learn more about the layout of the estate. He knew where he wanted to be, but he wasn't quite sure how to get there. Oliver used his smart phone's navigation to find Keenan's road. He then imposed a satellite image over the map to get a lay of the land.

As he had seen previously, beyond the houses were en-block garages, Oliver knew that much. But behind them was a large wooded area. With the location on the map, and the cursor showing his current location, Oliver was soon able to find where he needed to be.

Keenan's road looked completely different in the daylight. There were still a lot of parked vehicles along the full length of the road. This suggested that either not many people who lived here actually worked, or it was an affluent enough area where the partners could stay at home and they could afford two cars. Oliver concluded that the former was most likely the case as opposed to the latter.

The houses were set back from the road behind a narrow, tree-lined grassed verge. The trees themselves were throwing a blanket of shadow and coolness over the street.

Oliver started to feel a chill as he made his way down the street. Was it because of the shade afforded him by the trees, or was it his sinister motives for being there?

He walked the entire length of the street, on the opposite side from Keenan. He kept walking without breaking his stride, or even giving Keenan's house a purposeful glance. He wasn't interested in his house, not this time. All he noticed as he approached the house, was that the vehicle that was parked outside that evening was *not* there now. He continued beyond Keenan's house and into the area of the garages. The garaged area consisted of two opposing rows of ten garages, with a small turning area beyond them. The turning area was enclosed by fencing, but it had a hole made into it which led to the wooded area behind. Oliver felt that local children had created this over the years as a cut-through, or to be able to play in the woods.

Only when he was at the far end of the garages did he turn to look back towards the houses. From where he stood, Keenan's house was completely obscured by one of the blocks of garages. Oliver then kept close to the line of garages on the same side as Keenan's house. He then walked back towards the houses to see how close he could get whilst still keeping relatively out of sight.

Even without any cars parked within the garages, Oliver was able to walk the entire length of the garages, back towards the houses, without drawing attention to himself. Someone would have to be physically on the road themselves in order to see him.

Oliver looked at his watch, it was just before three o'clock in the afternoon. He felt that things were going to start getting busy shortly as the afternoon school run was about to begin. He felt there was nothing more he needed to achieve in the street. It was time to find out where the hole in the fence led to.

Oliver stepped through the stretched gap in the chicken wire fence. He stepped through it, then back again, then through it once more. He found it to be easy for him to fit through. But, he wanted to know if he could do it on the run. *There's a thought,* he pondered. Would he *even* be able to find the hole in a hurry, in darkness? That would need to be established in time. For now, Oliver just wanted to see where crossing the wooded area would bring him out.

As he went further into the woods it dawned on him just how dark and virtually impassable these woods would be at night. He had a head torch that he used for running, but there was no discernible or defined route through the woods. There were a couple of worn tracks, but again, Oliver was concerned that in his haste he may take a wrong turn after dark and get himself completely turned around and lost.

Eventually, having followed what he felt was the most defined and well used route through the wooded area, he came out onto the back of a car park, which in turn led out onto a road of business premises just off the High Street. As Oliver walked along this street the sun was to his back. For a moment the angles met and the sun's rays hit the reflector on the back of a parked car as he passed by it. The reflection hit him directly in the eyes and caused him to wince. It was then that an idea hit him, in this case literally.

On his way home, Oliver ensured that his route took him past an auto-repair shop. Inside he bought a pack of small orange reflectors. These were intended to mark the extremities of a driveway to enable safe manoeuvring at night, but were also perfect for Oliver's intended purpose for them.

oOo

Having come off his detour Oliver took the same route bus home.

As he entered through the front door, and much like this morning, the first thing to strike him was the aroma of something cooking; it wasn't immediately obvious to him what it was, but it did smell good.

"Ah, perfect timing," his father said as he saw him.

Oliver took off his coat and hung it in the hallway as he passed through into the kitchen.

He looked at a saucepan on the hob, it had reduced down by about an inch given the high tide mark on the pan. It wasn't really *perfect timing* at all, his father had just kept it simmering there until Oliver eventually came in, whatever time that would be. Oliver certainly wasn't going to point this out. It was a lovely gesture, and they were both going to make the best of it.

Once they were both sat down, it was his father who first started to talk. "So how was your day, did you get enough sleep?"

"Yeah, I'm shattered but got enough," Oliver replied. "I'll sleep well enough tonight. I just hopped the bus into town for a couple of things. How about you?"

"A bus, oh bugger, something wrong with your car?" his father exclaimed. "Sorry about that, I had to meet a client today, otherwise I'd have given you a lift."

He paused to take a mouthful of his dinner. It was a sausage casserole, a very overdone sausage casserole that was very chewy. As a result, his father's mouthful was taking longer than anticipated to get through. He ended up speaking through the final bits of it. "We'll try and sort you a car when this job is done, okay? I should be able to go halves with you."

"There's nothing wrong with my car, I chose to get the bus. It's cool, really," Oliver replied.

For him, there was no rush, and besides, his mind was elsewhere at the moment.

Chapter Fourteen

The next day Oliver woke up feeling fresh, having had a good night's sleep. He had slept in, so woke to find himself alone in the house.

It took so long for him to eventually get out of bed that breakfast soon became lunch, and it was nearly two o'clock by the time he had begun making preparations for the day.

Some of the things he was going to need he was able to immediately lay his hands on, whilst other things were a little more problematic to locate.

The hardest thing to find was his running head torch. He hadn't used it for a long time, so had absolutely no idea where to look for it. He ended up stumbling across it by chance when he went in search of a screwdriver which was needed to help with the reflectors he had bought the previous day. He found the head torch whilst rummaging through the toolbox. It was then he remembered having last used it in yet another need to do a repair on his car.

Oliver then thought that a screwdriver from a multi-tool was even more innocuous, certainly more so than a screwdriver or a hammer and nails, if ever he had to explain his possession of them.

Eventually, he had everything he felt he would need. They were all small items, easy enough to hide, and readily disposable and easy enough to discard should the need arise.

Oliver started reciting a list of all the items he had accumulated; "Reflectors and screws, yep, multi-tool, yep, head torch," he paused to turn it on then off again, "working, yep, gloves, yep, snood, yep." He then tailed off saying the last of the items verbally, having seen them in the bottom of his rucksack.

He was prepared but was he ready? There was plenty of time to get ready. He headed out.

It was a ten-minute bus ride today, shorter than the previous day. Oliver chose to pay his fare like everyone else this time too. He was focused on the task at hand, and didn't want any unexpected eventuality forcing him to detract from his plan. This was if something kicked off on the bus he could choose to ignore it and get off at the next stop. No one would be any the wiser, and certainly not aware of his status.

He intentionally got off the bus a few stops earlier so he would have to walk what was probably the last half mile to the High Street. From there he turned into the same side street again, and from there into the car park. However, this time, and in this direction, Oliver was on the lookout for any council operated CCTV cameras. Anything that covered public areas. Oliver already knew that most of the CCTV produced by shops and businesses was of very poor quality, but more importantly that it didn't cover public areas. It was allowed to extend a short distance beyond the boundary of the premises, but not to cover unnecessary public areas.

Oliver didn't think there was any CCTV, but until now he hadn't really been paying any specific attention. Now he had a reason to, now he *was* paying attention.

Oliver entered the car park as he had left it the previous day. He looked around the perimeter of the car park to see if there were any other exits. He couldn't see any. He didn't want to spend too much time on this task as he was conscious that anyone seeing a teenage male hanging around a car park is most likely casing cars to break into. Oliver didn't enter the car park until he had to. But the perimeter showed only one vehicular access. There was a secondary pedestrian access, which was a service alley between two shops on the High Street. Oliver ruled this out straight away as when he walked the length of the alleyway he saw CCTV for one of the premises covering their side door.

From the car park, Oliver went back into the wooded area. He found that just entering from the other side of the woods made it very disorientating. Initially, he couldn't find the same route back to the hole in the fence. But once eventually there, he stood with his back to the hole and walked forward until he was standing in front of the first tree that was in line with the hole.

Oliver then stood with his back to this tree and crouched down. From here he could see through the hole in the fence; beyond that, he could see between the line of garages and out into Keenen's road. Oliver estimated this to be a combined distance of about 50-60 metres. He then slipped off his rucksack and turned to face the tree again.

Oliver then used his multi-tool to screw one of the round orange reflectors to the tree at about waist height. He then crouched down again to place his head and eye line level with the reflector. Again, he looked back towards Keenan's road. Oliver felt confident that if he could see the road from here, then he would be able to see here from the road. He pressed on.

Oliver's next task was to familiarise himself with the quickest route back to the car park. It was more recognisable in this direction, and he was able to quickly find the same route he had used the previous day. He retraced it several times. Then once he was confident with the route he stood just inside of the hole in the fence. He then visualised the route, picked a prominent tree on the first part of that route, kept his focus on it as he approached it and dropped a reflector at his feet as he reached the tree. From here, he turned in the now familiar direction and repeated the process, each time picking a prominent tree and marking it, before moving on to the next. Only once this was complete, and Oliver was emerging from the woods towards the car park, did he return to check his route and affix the reflectors to their trees using the multi-tool and a single screw for each.

It was getting late by the time Oliver had finished his task, but it was not late enough. It was getting dark, but it was not dark enough.

Oliver returned to the High Street and allowed himself some respite by enjoying a portion of chips and a can of lemonade. For a moment the reason he was there, and the reason he had worked so diligently that afternoon, had escaped him.

With his break over, it was back to the task at hand. Oliver knew he had taken meticulous steps in ensuring his markers were well placed but there was only ever going to be one way to know if they would work as intended.

Oliver had dressed in suitable attire for his activities. He was wearing training shoes, tracksuit trousers and a fleece over a t-shirt. He also had a beanie type hat, a snood around his neck and a thin pair of running gloves so as not to impede his dexterity.

Oliver didn't want to be seen to run down Keenan's road just to turn and run back again. So, instead, he walked back out onto the High Street and started running the route he had walked in the previous day. It was sufficiently dark that the head torch wouldn't appear out of place. He wore it, but wouldn't be turning it on until it was required.

Oliver jogged along the main road through the estate. He cautiously turned into Keenan's road, without changing his pace. Then seeing the road was clear he increased his pace. His eyes focused ahead of him. He continued beyond Keenan's house without turning his head. He did, however, notice that the truck was still absent. He continued up to the garages. He was about to switch the torch on to shine the beam at the hole in the fence, but he didn't need to. The light from the street lamps behind him was sufficient to cause a reflection from beyond the fence. Without breaking his stride, and ducking unnecessarily low, Oliver leapt through the hole. He then turned slightly to his left and turned the torch on. The beam caught the next reflector. He headed towards it, searching for the next one as he approached it. He then saw the next, course deviated, then the next, and the next…

Then in an instant, there was a moment of panic. Oliver was no longer chasing the orange reflectors he had planted in a wooded area to show him the way.

In that instant, he was in the back seat of a car, and the intermittent orange glow became that of hazard indicators. He found himself now sitting in the back of his mother's car. Parked in a lay-by. He was all alone. All of a sudden, he could hear screaming. He could hear cries for help. Then, as suddenly as they started, the voice was silenced. Oliver still felt as if he was sat in the back of his mother's car, he was strapped in, he was unable to move, unable to free himself, he was paralysed with fear. Then a face came out of the darkness towards him, it loomed closer to him. It was a face he immediately recognised, but it was a face he hadn't seen for a long time. It was the face of Marc Sullivan, the man convicted of murdering his mother.

Oliver then found himself sitting on the ground. He was back in the wood, he turned his head violently, he was trying to find a recognisable image amongst the woodland. All this resulted in were intermittent flashes across the last reflector placed ahead of him. This simple action triggering the flashback of what happened years before.

Oliver snatched the torch from his head to prevent the orange reflection existing any more. He sat there, in the darkness, for a moment before slowly and cautiously rising to his feet. He then made his way back to the car park. He was still chasing his breath and trying to come to terms with what had just happened to him. Not in all the years since his mother's murder, and during all the years of counselling and therapy, had he *ever* hallucinated any re-enactment of that night, or had Sullivan ever appeared to him in anything other than dreams.

Oliver stretched out his arms above his head as he paced the across the car park trying to calm himself and catch his breath.

Given what had just happened, Oliver quickly reassessed his options. His markers had worked perfectly. He felt confident in his abilities to make a quick departure through the woods now, and he sure as hell wanted to make sure someone paid for how he was feeling.

Once he had his breath back, he looked at his watch, it was just after eight o'clock. From now on, what happened was going to be down to chance.

Oliver lapped around again. When he got back to the entrance to Keenan's road he stopped. From where he stood he could see that his truck was still yet to return. But everything else was in readiness.

There was a bus stop opposite the road. Had he known that, Oliver could have chosen to be dropped off here the previous day, but he needed to familiarise himself with this area, so walking the final part of the route was useful. Now he chose to wait. The bus shelter was of the chicane type, where you can enter at one end at the back, and exit at the other end to the front. The glass was filthy, and the interior light didn't work. But it was out of the wind, and it had seats, so it would be a perfect place for Oliver to wait in relative comfort. He sat, and he waited, and as he waited he watched, and he listened to music through one earpiece from headphones to his mobile phone.

Because this was the main road through the estate, there was no shortage of vehicles passing by. This was increasingly frustrating for Oliver as he was turning his head back and forth continuously. So, in order to calm himself, he sat with his head bowed, eyes ahead, barely open, he had turned the music down, so now he listened. He breathed deeply, calming himself.

He couldn't be sure how long he had continued to wait, for when the white crew-cab tipper came into view, looking at his watch was the last thing Oliver thought of doing. This appeared to be the same vehicle that Dave and Oliver had seen parked outside Keenan's house on the night that Keenan decorated their unmarked police car.

It had approached from Oliver's right, and made the slow turn into the side road with no indication.

Oliver had his headphones off in an instant. He tucked the cables away inside his fleece. He then stepped out of the bus shelter and crossed over the road and followed the tipper truck down the road. It was a tight fit for the truck given that there were now parked cars on both sides of the road.

Oliver felt confident that the truck would need to turn around in the turning circle beyond the garages before parking up. As it progressed down the road Oliver had put his beanie on, he had also pulled his snood up over his mouth and nose. Finally, he pulled on his gloves as he was jogging. Everything else was in his rucksack, except for what he needed next, and these items were in his pockets. He patted himself down to check they were where he was expecting them to be.

There was a parking space in front of Keenan's house. The question now was, would he just park up, or would he turn around before parking? Oliver was banking on the fact that he would turn around first, much like he had done previously. This would place the driver's side into the road, into the darkness of the street. This was what Oliver was banking on, and had factored into his plan.

The tipper truck slowed as it passed Keenan's house. Oliver stopped in his tracks. Was it just going to park? Then it started to move away again. Moving slowly towards the garages, the only available place to turn a vehicle of this size around in the street.

Because it slowed it did allow Oliver the chance to see into the cab through the rear windscreen. The driver, presumably Keenan, was the only person in it.

Oliver had decided that he would ambush the driver as he alighted from the cab when he had parked in front of the house. He meant to hold back, to hide behind a parked car opposite, to wait for the truck to turn around and park. Yet he found himself being drawn after the truck as it made its way along the length of the garages.

Oliver kept close to the garages to his left, off to the nearside of the truck. Once beyond the garages, the truck pulled around to the left, but did not have sufficient room to make a full turn in one manoeuvre. The reverse light then came on. Oliver darted across the width of the garages, passing behind the truck, below the view of the driver. The truck continued to reverse into the recess on the opposite side. It stopped to change out of reverse gear.

In that split second, when the vehicle was motionless, Oliver ran for the driver's door. He saw Keenan through the window. He snatched open the door and punched Keenan in the side of the neck before he even had a chance to turn his head. The punch impacted the Brachial Plexus, the network of nerves that send signals from the brain to the body. An impact to this area, called the Brachial Stun, *can* cause unconsciousness, but is a very effective strike to temporarily disable an opponent. It worked, Keenan fell limp and slumped forward in his seat.

Oliver then realised he wasn't wearing a seatbelt, so lowering him from the cab to the ground was fairly easy. Oliver let his body drop but protected him from injury by solely holding his right arm and his head.

In his torchlight Oliver confirmed it to be Keenan before he did anything else. For a moment, there was silence. No one had come to investigate. Oliver rolled Keenan onto his front. His arms pinioned below his body. Oliver turned Keenan's head to one side. Oliver then sat his bodyweight down on Keenan's lower back. This pressure, coupled with the fact that Oliver was straddling Keenan, meant that he couldn't free his arms from beneath him. However, Oliver had both arms free as they were not needed to restrain Keenan.

From his pockets, Oliver then took two items. One was once a large paperclip; the other was a domestic crème brûlée blowtorch. Oliver checked to see that his subject was still unconscious. He sparked the blowtorch into life. He then held the purple flame to the reshaped paperclip, which caused wisps of orange to shoot out. The paperclip started to glow red hot.

"Face or hand," Oliver muttered, as if he still had a choice to make. "Don't want this fucker getting away with it by wearing gloves now, do we?"

With that, he turned the blowtorch off and set it down on the ground beside him. He then cupped his gloved hand over Keenan's mouth before pressing the reshaped end of the paperclip against Keenan's left cheek.

Keenan immediately burst into life, but was unable to make a sound as Oliver's gloved hand stifled his screams of agony. He was also unable to move as his arms were trapped beneath him. He was helpless. Oliver could feel Keenan writhe and struggle beneath him. A dancing plume of smoke rose from his face along with the unmistakable stench of burning flesh. Keenan had to lay there and endure the unspeakable agony of having his face branded, and helpless to either prevent it from happening or even cry for help.

After only about a second of pressure, Oliver removed the branding iron. He took his hand from Keenan's mouth, he immediately started screaming in pain. Oliver then pushed down on the back of Keenan's shoulders to give himself assistance in standing up and a head start in getting away. Once standing, Oliver grabbed the blowtorch from where he had left it, and he was gone.

By the time Keenan was able to get to his feet, his attacker was nowhere in sight.

Chapter Fifteen

Oliver's next shift back on duty was an early shift, a seven a.m. start. He met with Dave and his colleagues for a cup of tea prior to the briefing.

At the appointed hour they filed into the briefing room. Their Sergeant was sitting at a desk with a computer workstation on it. They all took seats facing a projector screen.

Having been given their call-signs for the shift, as well as any assigned tasks, the briefing then consisted of several projected slides showing recent incidents, as well as known offenders habits, and requests for intelligence on certain subjects.

When one slide came up, Oliver felt a chill engulf him. He recognised the man in the slide, and he recognised his handiwork. It was Keenan.

The slide showed two facial images; the image on the left was how everyone knew Keenan, it showed the custody 'mug-shot' from his most recent custody visit. The other image was hardly recognisable to be the same person. The face was swollen and bruised and bloodied. On the left cheek was a large discolouration. At first glance, it couldn't be determined if it was a scab or charring.

A murmur of disgust and displeasure initially fell across the room. Oliver remained unwavering and silent.

The Sergeant then began to read the text on the screen below the images. "Yesterday, Ryan Keenan presented himself to hospital with the above injuries. The attack took place outside his home address at approximately 8.30 p.m. the previous evening. He was not able to describe his attackers, or provide a motive. Any information to CID quoting the incident reference."

Oliver started to give thought to the word on the slide, *attackers*, after all, it was only him there. He wondered what Keenan had reported.

"It wasn't us, Sarge, I promise you that," said a voice from a row behind Oliver. It raised a chuckle.

"All right, all right, knock it off guys, I know we all like to raise a smile when some shit gets what's coming to him, but this could be the start of something bigger, just keep your eyes open, okay," the Sergeant concluded.

oOo

After briefing, Oliver was sitting at a computer terminal. The terminal he had chosen, and the way he was sitting at it, meant he could see anyone approach him in good time. He could see Dave approaching him. Oliver quickly exited the program he was viewing and returned to his email account screen.

"The Sarge needs a word," Dave said.

"Do you know what it's about?" Oliver replied.

"Something to do with Keenan…"

Oliver felt the colour drain from his face. Oliver's first instinct was to immediately consider *that* night.

"When you nicked him; he's making a complaint."

Oliver felt his heart begin to slow, mercifully before it burst out of his chest. It wasn't to do with the briefing slide at all.

"Do you want me in there with you?" Dave asked. As Oliver's mentor, Dave had overall responsibility for Oliver.

Essentially Oliver's decisions were not his own to make, Dave had the final word on anything they actioned.

oOo

"Have a seat, Oliver," the Sergeant said. "Are you sitting in on this too, Dave?"

"If that's okay?" Dave replied.

"If that's what Oliver wants?" the Sergeant asked, looking at Oliver, who nodded his approval.

"Okay, let's get on with it. Oliver," he paused in order to get to the correct part of the report he needed to refer to, "a complaint has come in from a Mister Ryan Keenan. He states that when you arrested him you were heavy-handed. Now, I've read your arrest statement *and* the *Use of Force* form, and I'm happy with both. But, the nature of the complaint is a serious one, and it does need to be investigated."

The Sergeant looked at Oliver, as if he expected some kind of reaction or at the very least a verbalised response. Dave looked at Oliver, expecting the same. Both were disappointed. The room was silent.

The Sergeant continued, "Now, I've spoken to the Inspector. We are in agreement that we feel Keenan is just pissed off at having his arse handed to him a couple of days ago and he's looking to have a go at anyone he can. This complaint only came in when we went to see him at the hospital. But that said, there is potentially a legitimate case here, and we need to be seen to act appropriately. Keenan didn't mention anything at the time, so that's in our favour, *but* he is pissed off and is capable of making this into something it isn't."

They both saw Oliver nod along.

"Oliver, I'm gonna have to put you on restricted duties until this is all dealt with, okay? That means office based duties only, no direct contact with the public, nothing in custody, nothing in the front office. Dave will still be your mentor, but you'll now be directly responsible to me."

The Sergeant then turned to face Dave. "You can go out on solo patrol until this is all sorted out, okay? All right, we're done here then."

Both Dave and Oliver got up. Dave stepped towards the door and held it open for Oliver who nodded in gratitude as he walked through it with his head bowed.

"C'mon, let's grab a coffee," Dave suggested.

Within a few minutes they were perched on the back of the sofas that furnished the canteen area.

Oliver took a sip from his mug.

"It's a good thing Sarge didn't see that, or you'd have had some explaining to do."

Oliver looked puzzled. "See *what?*"

"That!" Dave said, pointing towards the hand that Oliver was holding his mug with.

Oliver passed the mug to his left hand and looked at what Dave was referring to. The knuckles on the back of his right hand were bruised and swollen.

"What happened, what did you hit?" Dave asked.

"Ah, it was something stupid. I just get a little upset sometimes," Oliver explained.

"Well, that's hardly surprising given all that you've been through. Just try and keep a lid on it, okay, and certainly don't go getting *upset* again this side of any ruling." Dave pleaded.

"I'll do my best," Oliver replied. "So, what am I gonna be doing in the office all day?"

"Anything and everything," Dave replied. "You'll be the team's Baldrick, a dogsbody, any grimy little admin tasks need doing, you'll be doing them. Misper enquiries, y'know, like phoning round the hospitals and stuff like that, that'll be you. Don't worry, there'll be plenty to keep you busy."

"Great," replied Oliver, with more than a hint of sarcasm.

A *misper*, or missing person, is an investigation into someone whose whereabouts are unknown. Initially, it can be as simple and straightforward as making direct contact with them or attending an address. But quite often the enquiries become protracted and involve broader and more random enquiries, such as phoning local hospitals for any admissions in the missing person's name. This would be where Oliver would prove useful.

"Don't go getting too engrossed in any of that stuff just yet though, you're gonna have to fill out a couple of forms in response to the complaint first," Dave concluded.

oOo

After their coffee, Oliver returned to his desk. He unlocked his terminal to see an email from his Sergeant.

'Oliver, fill out these forms as best you can, Dave can help, get them back to me ASAP' the mail read. It also contained numerous attachments.

Much as Dave had predicted, he had sent Oliver forms to complete to allow him to respond to the complaint that had been made against him.

In order to provide an accurate account for the report, Oliver needed to review his arrest statement and the incident log. He needed to ensure his timeline was accurate, and that his report didn't conflict with anything that had already been documented.

The reports didn't take anywhere near as long as Oliver was led to believe. He finished them in good time. But chose not to return them to his Sergeant until he had progressed with something else first. The *something else* was what he had minimised and hidden from Dave when he had approached his desk earlier.

Oliver felt as long as his Sergeant thought he was busy doing something he'd asked of him, then there was less chance of him being disturbed, or tasked with anything else. Oliver had reopened the screen he had shut down when Dave first approached him prior to the meeting. Once again, this had his full attention. But unlike before, there was now even less chance of being interrupted.

The situation that Oliver now found himself in, being on restricted duties, wasn't nearly as bleak as Dave had made it out to be. Oliver felt he needed some time out of the watchful eye of his mentor, where every move was under scrutiny.

He liked Dave, he really did, but what he needed to do, he couldn't do whilst being watched. For Oliver, the task now at hand was far more important.

Chapter Sixteen

A couple of weeks had passed. The investigation into Oliver's complaint of excessive force during the arrest of Ryan Keenan was ongoing. He was still on restricted duties.

Also, in this time another briefing slide had been produced. Similar to the one showing Ryan Keenan and the injuries that he had sustained. This one showed another local yob, Louis Patterson-Grey, someone who fancied himself as a bit of a gangster, or should that read *gangsta*, despite his regal sounding name. Again, the slide showed the team a number of images of Patterson-Grey; the first being his most recent custody photo, the second showing a bruised and beaten man who was barely recognisable as the same person. The third showed a close up of a cleaned facial injury. The Sergeant read aloud the caption below this image on the slide. "A letter 'F' has been branded into his left cheek."

A voice raised from the team, "What does 'F' stand for?"

"Fuck knows," came a reply. "Fuck, that hurts," said someone else. These witticisms raised a chuckle amongst the team.

"Okay, knock it off, guys," the Sergeant interjected, "this is pretty serious, this is the second one of these in the last month. They've had a closer look at what happened to Oliver and Dave's buddy Keenan, and they've determined that he was branded too. It looks like we've got someone hitting some of our major players, and at the moment CID have got absolutely nothing to link these incidents. They don't roll together, so they don't know why these two would be targeted in similar fashion."

The Sergeant scanned the rows of uniformed officers sitting before him. He could see Dave, but he couldn't see Oliver.

"Has anyone seen Oliver," he asked. He then looked across the office to see Oliver enter through the door at the far end. The Sergeant's moment of genuine concern quickly turned to agitation.

"Nice of you to join us, Oliver, you're very nearly *almost* on time," he said with an increasingly sarcastic tone.

Oliver was only a few minutes late. He was hoping the Sergeant didn't need to make any bigger deal about it than he had already done. To avoid disrupting the proceedings any further, Oliver remained at the back of the room. He was unaware of the contents of the briefing as it was concluded following his Sergeant's sarcastic sentiment.

Oliver again found himself a workstation away from any other officers. The office was crowded, there were still a few officers working from the off-going night shift, as well as those from his team. As per his new routine on restricted duties, he would busy himself checking his email and reviewing his workload until he was tasked with anything required of him that day.

It had only been a couple of weeks since the complaint had come in and since he had been put on restricted duties, but he was already feeling isolated and to some extent ostracised from the rest of the team.

A short while later, Dave came over. Oliver didn't see him approach and was startled when Dave greeted him. "Morning, how's you?"

This flustered Oliver in a way that Dave had never seen before. His eyes were on Oliver, so he didn't catch any glimpse of what was on the screen which Oliver so hastily minimised on realising he was no longer alone.

"No need to shit yourself, I'm only saying hey," Dave said.

Having composed himself, Oliver struggled to find a suitable reply. People were used to him remaining silent, he felt that was the best response.

"Sarge is asking for you to call up and have some checks done on this address before we make an arrest attempt." Feeling that Oliver may need to have that request elaborated on, he continued. "Just call up Control and ask for checks to be run on the address and any persons linked to it, okay?"

Dave held out a piece of paper for Oliver, it had the address they were going to attend, as well as the person they were looking to arrest.

The checks that Oliver had been asked to carry out were to make all officers going to make the arrest aware of any warnings that anyone there may have. These may include violence, officer safety (known to attack officers or resist arrest), weapons, drugs (likelihood of needles at the address, or have psychopathic tendencies), as well as anything else anyone there may be wanted in connection with.

As Dave held out the piece of paper, Oliver reached up a hand which had been clasped with the other in his lap.

As he extended his hand into view Dave could see fresh abrasion injuries across the back of his hand, pronounced swelling across his knuckles.

Oliver took hold of the piece of paper and began to retract his hand. Dave held fast. Both hands started to tremble under the tension. Oliver turned to face Dave.

It was then that Dave saw that the injuries weren't localised to Oliver's hands. He had haemorrhaging around his right eye.

In shock, Dave let go of the paper, Oliver's hands disappeared back beneath the table.

Dave crouched down so he was hidden behind the table and computer monitor. He spoke in a whisper to best ensure that no one in the busy office would hear them.

"What the fuck happened to you?" Dave asked.

"I've started up karate again," came the reply.

"Again? I didn't know you did karate, my kids go local. How long you been doing that?"

"Not long, did it when I was younger, Dad wanted me to do it," Oliver replied.

Dave poked his head above the height of the computer monitor, he had a good look around the office before ducking back down again.

"Look, you're already up against the wall with this Keenan complaint, yeah we know it's bullshit. It's like the Sarge says, he's just pissed off coz he got a pasting, and he's looking to pay it forward. It's gonna blow over if you keep your head down, but not if you keep turning up for work 'A' late and 'B' with injuries! You see where I'm coming from?"

There was no response from Oliver, but Dave was fairly sure his message had sunk in. Dave rose to his feet. He looked around the office, no one was within earshot.

"Let us know when you get the results of the checks will ya," he said as his parting remark.

Chapter Seventeen

Once again Oliver found himself in the Sergeant's office.

"They've made an initial ruling on the complaint, Oliver. There is going to be a formal investigation."

Oliver just sat there, appearing to be unfazed by what had just been said to him. The Sergeant felt as if more clarification was required.

"Due to the nature of the allegation against you, you are going to be suspended from duty until a formal hearing convenes to rule on it. Oliver, you're still a probationer, you could lose your job over this. This *is* serious. And, Oliver, you haven't exactly done yourself any favours in the meantime either." He paused, frustrated with the apparent insolence he was being confronted with. Oliver was showing no signs of remorse or regret in any way.

"Since this complaint came in you've been late on several occasions, granted it's never been by that much, but it's the principle of things, you've got to be whiter than white at times like this. You're covered with scrapes and bruises. Yeah, I've seen them, you try hard not to have them on show, wearing a bloody fleece in the office, c'mon who are you fooling? Are you gonna tell me where these injuries have come from? And don't tell me it's from karate becau…"

In an instant, Oliver lost all interest in what his Sergeant had to say. After all the little speeches about being able to trust him, and 'what's said in the car, stays in the car' and ensuring that no one was in earshot for his little pep-talks, in an instant, Oliver realised that his colleague and mentor Dave was actually full of shit. As likely to betray his trust and go squealing to their Sergeant as much as the next officer.

Oliver flashed back to the evening that he and Dave had parked up outside Keenan's, when he actually thought he was on the same page as Dave, when Dave suggested doing Keenan, and he was about to readily agree.

People often thought of Oliver as being rude for being so quiet, and not responding to everything that was said to him. A quiet child is considered shy and endearing, a quiet teenager is considered rude or insolent. Oliver liked that just fine.

"If you don't want to tell me now, you don't have to. But, just be prepared to be able to explain and justify them to the disciplinary panel, okay?"

Explain what? Oliver thought. He knew he had entirely missed what his Sergeant had just said to him. When in reality, his Sergeant was making reference to his recent injuries.

"Your suspension is effective immediately, I'm afraid. You'll need to collect everything you need and go home. You will no doubt be contacted by the Police Federation to arrange any representation." The Sergeant paused. "Just think long and hard about what you're gonna say, get your account straight in your mind. I'm sure you'll be fine. Is there anything you want to ask of me?"

Oliver just shook his head.

"We're done here then. Dave will see you out of the building. When you're outside he will need to take your warrant card from you. All the time you're on suspension, you're no longer a police officer."

The Sergeant said this in such a way, determined to get a reaction from Oliver, but just as so many had tried before him, he was left disappointed.

"How'd it go?" Dave asked on seeing Oliver exit the Sergeant's office. Oliver just shrugged.

"I hear you're being suspended as the complaint's going formal," he continued.

If you know, why ask? Oliver thought.

"I need to escort you from the building and take your warrant card from you," Dave said.

You don't have to be so fucking gleeful about it, Oliver continued thinking. He finally knew exactly where he stood with Dave. He had finally shown his loyalty. Oliver was just relieved that he hadn't disclosed anything to him he would've since regretted.

Dave walked with Oliver to watch him log off his computer. The office was virtually empty. There was certainly no one there that Oliver felt compelled to say goodbye to.

He was then escorted to his locker, where he hung up his uniform fleece and retrieved his jacket from a hanger. Oliver didn't mind the scrutiny that Dave afforded him. He had nothing to take from his locker apart from his personal possessions. Dave watched what he took, there was nothing that he had to challenge, or that concerned him. It was there that he took Oliver's warrant card from him. Oliver wouldn't need it in order to exit the building as Dave would now be escorting him.

From the locker room, Dave led them both downstairs and outside. He held out his hand for Oliver to shake. For a moment Oliver looked down at it, he took a moment to consider his options. Then he shook it.

"I'll see you soon, call me at home if you need anything," Dave offered as a parting gesture.

Not bloody likely, Oliver thought. But nonetheless, he smiled, and walked away.

Chapter Eighteen

As Oliver was now suspended from work he had to decide what explanation to give to his father as to why he was going to be at home every day for the foreseeable future.

With all the other deceit and cloak and dagger activities, Oliver couldn't face fabricating yet another lie, not to his father. So, the following morning, over breakfast he came clean. In truth, he felt there was nothing to feel ashamed about. He admitted to intentionally being a little heavy-handed when it came to the arrest of Keenen, although he didn't mention him by name. Oliver also mentioned that Keenan had recently taken a beating and that his Sergeant thought that Keenan was making the complaint just because he was seeking any form of retribution he could.

His father agreed with the Sergeant's remarks. He did, however, add, "When will you *ever* learn? This is just like the karate class all over again. I was hoping you joining the police would've quelled that side of you, just looks like it's given you even *more* opportunities."

Oliver's father certainly had a point. At the end of the day, it came down to cause and effect. His over-zealous and heavy-handed approach towards the arrest of Keenan came as a direct result of being in the presence of someone as malevolent as him.

Oliver saw Keenan as someone without a conscience. He felt that someone who preyed on the trusting and vulnerable couldn't possibly ever see the error of their ways, and as a result could never be rehabilitated. Keenan, like so many others, was just plain evil.

The only other thing that Oliver's father asked, was what he was going to do with the time he now had off work.

"I'm not sure really. Was thinking about some time away. I don't have a hearing date yet, so I don't wanna go abroad or anything. Maybe I'll take a trip up north or something."

"Well, if you need a few quid to go and enjoy yourself with, then let me know," his father said.

Firstly, there was no *maybe* about any of it, this was the first lie he had openly told his father. Oliver had been preparing for the eventuality of being suspended. Secondly, he had been squirrelling away a portion of his salary each month. In the time he had been in the police he had saved almost £5,000. It was sitting in cash in a shoebox on a shelf in his wardrobe.

He wasn't quite sure what he was going to need the money for yet, but he certainly didn't need his father to lend him any.

"Just try and not get yourself into any more trouble between now and the hearing, that's the last thing you need," his father included as an addendum.

oOo

During the time Oliver had been on restricted duties in the office, he still managed to be a productive and useful member of the team. He had taken on numerous tasks to relieve his colleagues of them. He was also able to progress both his, and others' investigations by making telephone enquiries, arranging for CCTV to be downloaded and ready to be collected, as well as the numerous, onerous misper enquiries.

But despite this, Oliver had been busy to his own ends. He had an agenda, tasks that needed to be fulfilled. This took precedence over anything he was asked, or assigned to do.

Oliver had spent a significant amount of time in the office conducting research. Whilst in the office he had access to databases he would never have elsewhere.

By his own admission to his father, he was heavy-handed in the arrest of Keenan. But this was not as a punishment for Keenan's heinous acts against the vulnerable. This had, in fact, the sole intention of raising a complaint and getting Oliver placed on restricted duties. Because, once on restricted duties, he would have the luxury of time and relative privacy to do what he needed to do.

Had Keenan not made the complaint, then Oliver would've simply sought out further means to rock the boat and get him placed on restricted duties. He had a back-up plan of feigning an illness or injury, but assaulting Keenan was just too good an opportunity to pass up.

Once again, Oliver had the luxury of time. He would be advised of the date of his hearing in due course, but until then, his time was his own.

oOo

"Off out so soon?" his father called out at seeing Oliver coming down the stairs carrying what appeared to be a full rucksack.

"Yeah, I'm just gonna have a couple of nights away, y'know, clear my head a bit," Oliver replied.

"Okay, well you be careful," his father said as Oliver came up and hugged him. He then walked back down the hallway.

"What's with the baseball cap?" his father asked.

"Oh, it's bright outside, I can't find my sunglasses," came the reply.

"Oh, I thought you were hiding from something," his father joked.

Oliver smiled as he opened the front door, and left.

His father was expecting to hear Oliver's car start up and pull out of the driveway, but instead, there was silence. After a moment, he went to the front door. He opened it, expecting to see Oliver with the car, maybe experiencing the continued troubles he was having with it. But no, the car was there, next to his on the driveway, and Oliver was nowhere to be seen. Wherever he had gone, he had gone on foot.

oOo

Oliver had walked to the rail station. He knew exactly where he wanted to go. He had the route already planned out. But he didn't buy a ticket for the entire journey, and certainly not a return ticket. The journey would require him to change trains twice. Oliver had bought a single ticket from his home station to the first change station only. From there, he would buy a ticket for the next part of his journey, and so on. Also, he intended to pay for his tickets with cash.

Chapter Nineteen

Oliver took a lot longer than necessary to reach his destination. This was, however, intentional. Today, he wasn't in any hurry. He had left the station each time he was required to change train. He took the time to walk around the town, he had a coffee at one stop, and some lunch at the other. By the time he had reached his final destination it was getting dark, and he was hungry again.

But first things first, Oliver needed to secure accommodation for the night, nothing had been pre-booked. He wandered a few streets near to the rail station until he found what he was looking for.

He had checked himself into a Bed and Breakfast hotel, one that was cheap, and not in any way luxurious, but adequate for his needs.

He was in the room long enough to dump his bag down and use the toilet. Then, he was off out again. Only this time he knew exactly where he was heading. He was heading across town, geographically it was less than two miles away. Again, Oliver walked the route, taking into consideration landmarks, cut-throughs and alleyways.

It was dark by the time Oliver reached the road he was in search of, Allingham Road. It was a wide tree-lined road consisting of substantial detached properties which were once single dwellings that had been mostly converted into flats. This was only evident as the front gardens of those converted had been partially, if not fully, paved to allow for a number of cars to be parked on them. Far more than any single-family dwelling would normally need.

The distance that the front of the buildings was from the pavement made seeing the door numbers difficult. Oliver was only able to see random numbers here and there. From what he could see, he knew he was on the correct side of the road, and heading in the right direction.

Oliver found the building he needed, number 46; this was found more by a process of elimination than from seeing the correct door number. Unlike the majority of the buildings on the street, this was a purpose-built block of flats. Oliver surveyed it from the street. It was an architectural monstrosity compared to some of the Edwardian houses that he had passed along the street to get there.

From the street, Oliver could see that the building consisted of four floors. There was no sign of an entrance from the street; Oliver concluded it must be down the right side, along the wider of the two side passages that he could see, also this was the only side that was somewhat illuminated. The car park in front of the building only had spaces for eight to ten cars. The bays weren't marked, so Oliver was guessing the capacity based on considerate parking. Not nearly enough parking for the block, unless the building only consisted of two flats per floor, which Oliver seriously doubted.

Oliver walked across the car park and approached the left side of the building. He could see security lighting covering the car park and main side passage. But no CCTV cameras.

As Oliver approached the building itself he was able to see the depth of the property. It went back further than he initially thought. Given the revised dimensions, he considered that there would be possibly four to six flats per floor, giving a total of sixteen to twenty-four flats. There were lights on everywhere throughout the building. From what Oliver knew about this building it was a halfway hostel for released offenders. Essentially, it was somewhere that prisoners who had been released could use as a temporary address until they got themselves established in their own right. Somewhere to have postal applications sent to until they could move on.

So, realising this about the residents of the building, he wasn't surprised to see that most of the flats were presently occupied.

As Oliver turned the corner onto the rear of the building, he realised the need for the second side passage. It gave the refuse collectors access to the bin storage area. That's why this passage was insecure, no gates across to make their job of retrieving the dumpsters easier. It also made what Oliver had in mind easier too.

The grounds behind the property weren't nearly as substantial as those set to the front. The building itself took up the vast majority of the plot. It had evidently been deemed that the intended clientele didn't have the need for a recreation space. All that occupied the rear grounds were a rotary clothesline and a hexagonal picnic table.

Oliver walked the entire width of the rear of the building without any security lights coming on. From the final corner of the building, he looked up. Above him was a security light, but for whatever reason it didn't come on as he passed under it.

Oliver headed back towards the street along the wide side passage. He approached a recess. Within this recess was the front door. The doors were aluminium and glass and looked as if they came from a 1980s bank frontage. Oliver tried the door. It was locked. There wasn't a touchpad for a fob or card, the residents must have to use a key to gain entry. Next to the door was an entry-com system.

Its button box consisted of three columns of ten buttons. Next to each button was a small label, some had legible numbers on them, but most didn't. Oliver didn't have a flat number, all he had was the address, and he had followed that as far as he could. He knew he was at the right building as he could finally see a street number adjacent to the front door.

"A fat lot of good it is here," he said to himself, "who the fuck can see it here from the street?"

Oliver stepped back out of the recessed entrance and looked back towards the street. There was no one in sight. He then approached the front door. He tried it again, more vigorously than before. It was still secure. He then pressed his face towards the glass and cupped around his eyes to minimise the glare.

In the entrance lobby Oliver could see an ascending staircase ahead of him, and doors off to both sides. On the wall to his right was a wall-mounted shelf unit with cubby-holes. It appeared to be for the post for the individual flats. To the right of the front door, beneath the plaque with the building number on it, was the letterbox. Oliver could see through the lower glass panel that the post was delivered by dropping it onto the floor, and that someone then sorted it into the individual flats.

It was then that a pair of feet emerged at the top of the stairs ahead of him. Oliver had an idea. He exited the recess and disappeared out of sight back along the side passage, towards the street. He pulled his collar up high so that it covered a lot of his face. He poised himself ready to walk on the signal. He held his keys in his hand.

The signal was hearing the door open within the recess. Oliver then casually strolled into the recess to see the door opening inwards and a heavy-set man in a dark coat and woollen hat walk out. He ignored Oliver as he passed him, allowing the door to close by itself. Oliver then caught the door before it shut. He turned to see that the man was not yet out of sight. Oliver entered the lobby.

He quietly closed the door. He waited for a moment. Listening. Listening to the sounds coming from the flats, coming from the street. To all intents and purposes, he was alone. Inside the door was a round button, which if pressed would activate the lights in the lobby and stairwell for a short time. Oliver didn't activate it as he had sufficient light from the outside security lighting for what he needed to achieve.

He approached the wall-mounted shelf unit and started to look at the post for each flat. He was looking for the name Marc Sullivan. The man who was convicted of killing Oliver's mother nearly fifteen years earlier.

Oliver became increasingly frustrated as he went along the first row of cubby-holes without success, then the second, and finally exhausting the third. There was nothing in Sullivan's name.

Oliver looked around the lobby. He was hoping to see a notification of some kind, maybe giving a list of residents. Again, he was out of luck. He gave momentary consideration to going upstairs and wandering around each level in turn. *But to what end* he thought, *what would he be looking for?*

Oliver turned back towards the door, resigning himself to the fact that the information that brought him here may very well be out of date. That information was almost a year old, since Sullivan was released. After all, this was just intended to be a temporary release address, not a permanent placement. Oliver took hold of the door handle and began to turn it. He looked down in disappointment.

It was then that he saw the fresh mail on the floor just inside the front door. He hurriedly crouched down with renewed hope. He scooped it up and began sifting through it, and there it was. Amongst all the other letters and junk mail and leaflets was a single letter addressed to Mr M Sullivan, and giving the address of Flat 15, 46 Allingham Road. He let the other letters fall to the floor. He looked at the franking impression. It did not give any indication as to the sender, but it was dated two days earlier.

"You fucking bastard," Oliver said as he held the letter in his hands. "Flat fifteen."

Once again Oliver crouched down. He placed the letter amongst those that had fallen to the floor. He stood up and listened. Again, no one could be heard.

Oliver had a wander past the staircase. He wanted to get an idea of the layout of the building before venturing upstairs. The door to flat 1 was on his left before the staircase, flat 2 was beyond it on the same side. Flats 3 and 4 were opposite. As Oliver ascended the stairs he worked out that flat 15 must be on the top floor, towards the rear of the building.

Oliver made his way to the top floor without activating any of the timer light switches. It got darker as he got higher, as he was now above the fittings for the external security lighting. But he was able to see what he needed. Flat 15 was indeed on the top floor, in the far-left corner of the building as viewed from the street.

"Motherfucker," Oliver said, as he stood in front of the door to flat 15. He placed his knuckles against the door frame and lowered his head against the door, turning his head as he did. He listened. He couldn't hear anything coming from within the flat.

He looked around the landing. There were clear beams of light coming from beneath the doors to the other flats. Someone was home at each of them. Either no one was home at flat 15, or he was asleep, or had a draught excluder strip along the bottom of the door. Either way, this was the right door.

There was nothing more that Oliver could do here this evening. He had achieved everything he wanted to. He was grateful for that. Even if someone was home he wouldn't be acting any further, despite fighting the urge to do so.

As Oliver descended from the fourth to the third floor he heard footsteps coming up to meet him. In an instant there was a moment of indecision, and with that came panic. *What do I do?* He thought.

Oliver hesitated for a moment at the top of the stairs that led from the third to the second floor. He could now see a shadow emerging around the corner below him. Oliver could not make his legs work as he wanted to. If he passed this person he would now look out of place, gone was his fluid casual motion. He resorted to his only other option. He hid behind the staircase by the door to flat 10.

The shadow beneath him became a person and the person was coming up the stairs. With the exertion of climbing the stairs came a series of coughs from an out of shape man. Then he came into view.

It was the same man that Oliver had passed to gain access to the building. He hadn't put any lights on, so Oliver felt safe hiding in the shadows. He just kept his fingers crossed that he didn't live in flat 10.

He didn't, he turned back on him to climb the last flight to the fourth floor and disappeared out of sight. Oliver then heard a key turn in a lock, a door was heard to open, and then it closed.

Finally, he could hear a security chain be drawn across the back of the door. There was silence. Oliver's heart started to slow.

Fourth floor, locked flat, all the others were occupied when he was up there. Oliver wondered. He crept back to the fourth floor. He didn't leave the head of the stairs. He didn't need to. He could see what he needed to see from the stairs. There was now light coming from underneath the door of flat 15.

"You absolute fucking cunt!" Oliver muttered. A look of grim determination and hatred engulfed his face. In an instant, he realised that he had earlier come face-to-face with the man who had killed his mother, the reason he was here.

It took a moment or two for Oliver to compose himself after this unexpected revelation. He knew he should leave. He descended the stairs to see the pile of post strewn out over a wider area. He crouched down to confirm one thing. The letter addressed to Mr M Sullivan was no longer there. Oliver smiled triumphantly. He left through the front door and headed towards the rear of the building. He walked to the furthermost point of the rear grounds. He looked back at the building. He could now see lights on in what he believed to be flat 15. The curtains were now closed. He couldn't see anything going on within the flat.

"We're done for today," he said as he walked back out to the street. He was now in search of something to eat.

Chapter Twenty

Now that Oliver had found who he was looking for, and the added bonus of also having a pretty good idea of what Sullivan currently looked like, it was now a case of establishing his routines. To know where Sullivan was going to be and when.

Until then the only image Oliver had of Sullivan was the last custody photo that was taken when he was arrested prior to serving fourteen years for murder. He had changed, he'd aged badly, though thankfully not that much. But Oliver would need to see him in the daylight to be sure of any specific characteristics. For that, he would have to play the waiting game.

Oliver rose early the following day, before the breakfast that was included in his booking was served. He grabbed himself something on the go as he made his way back towards Allingham Road. He knew his destination this time, so he varied his route to make himself more familiar with the surrounding roads. It was useful that Sullivan's block only had access from the front. Oliver was able to wander the street periodically and still see the front edge of the car park, for any comings and goings.

He knew it was a ridiculous thing to expect himself to have eyes on the building continuously for the whole day. He knew he was playing the odds, hoping to get lucky. Oliver patrolled the street in front of the block for a couple of hours first thing in the morning, between eight and ten a.m., then again around lunchtime, and again in the afternoon. But he knew he had to be back at the same time as he had been there the previous evening.

Sullivan had only been out for about ten to fifteen minutes the night before. That was time enough to get to the nearest parade of shops and back. Oliver needed to know if he was a creature of habit. He hoped that the cough, and the smell as he passed him in the confines of the staircase, suggested he was a smoker, and one with quite a habit. A habit that hopefully required frequent topping up.

It became decidedly chilly once the sun descended below the tops of the buildings and Oliver, although prepared in the main, wasn't dressed to be outside for an extended period of time. He relinquished his position across from Sullivan's block and headed back towards the town for suitable refreshments and to warm up for the late shift.

oOo

Oliver was back in position with plenty of time to spare, well before the time he had been there the previous evening. On first arrival he had performed a recce around the back of the block of flats. This was redundant earlier in the day in broad daylight, as it wouldn't indicate anything. But now, in darkness again, it would be a good indicator of who was home and who wasn't. This was determinable by seeing lights on in the flats.

From his concealed vantage point under the trees at the furthest point from the building in the rear grounds, Oliver could see that the lights were on in Sullivan's flat. He was hoping that this was a good indicator that he was home. He was also hoping that as the lights were all off when Sullivan was out the previous evening this was another habit of his.

Oliver was far more comfortable where he now sat. He had relocated a discarded milk crate from where he had found it beside one of the dumpsters to its new location, beneath his backside, under the trees.

Although he was now somewhat comfortable, he was bored. He couldn't use his smartphone at all as the glare from the screen display would light him up like a Christmas tree. His boredom led to agitation. He sat there cursing Sullivan, "Come on, you fucker, go and get your fucking fags already!"

All Oliver could do now was sit and wait. He didn't need to be as hyper-vigilant as he was during the day. He now had the relative luxury of being able to relax, to a certain extent. He was able to go to the toilet amongst the bushes when needed and still keep an eye out for the lights in Sullivan's windows.

He found he was checking his watch with an almost obsessive frequency. Time, however, was virtually standing still for him. The time he had arrived there the previous day had now passed. This time yesterday, Oliver recalled, he was standing outside the front door when he saw Sullivan coming down the stairs. *If only he knew then what he knew now*, he thought.

His mind started to wander on that subject. What if he had known the man to pass him was Sullivan, the reason he had taken three trains and a stay in a B&B to be here? What would he have done? Would he have done anything? He wouldn't have been prepared for that in any case. It wouldn't have been part of the plan.

The plan... What plan? Oliver thought. He hadn't thought that far ahead. He hadn't even counted on getting as far as he had already, what with successfully tracking down and locating Sullivan. He had deliberately not planned beyond that for fear of losing focus on the task at hand.

But he now had Sullivan in hand. What should the next step be? Maybe it was time to consider the remainder of the plan.

Oliver felt he needed an endgame, and to then work backwards from it. He already had his final move in mind. That was what got him started on all this in the first place.

Oliver had enacted his end game in his mind countless times over the years. He had lived it, relived it, and refined it into a beautiful symphony of vengeance and attrition. Oliver had been tormented by Sullivan's face since that evening it was pressed against the glass of his mother's car window, when her silenced cries still echoed in his head, taunting him, haunting him.

Oliver could feel the rage building within him. He started to relive his recollection of that evening. The journey home, the upset and agitation in his mother's voice. The stop in the lay-by. The last time he saw her. The next person he saw. Sullivan.

For a moment, Oliver's concentration had wandered from the task in hand. He looked back at the windows of the top floor flat. The lights were no longer on.

Oliver panicked. He looked at his watch, nearly fifteen minutes had passed since he last looked at it. For almost fifteen minutes he had reminisced about his mother, and the night Sullivan took her from him, and what Oliver had schemed over the years to do to him if he ever had the opportunity. The opportunity that had now come knocking.

An opportunity that maybe Oliver had missed this evening. He stood up in a flash. He kept close to the treeline that marked the perimeter of the rear grounds. He ran around to the front door. He waited there for a few seconds. He waited long enough for what he thought someone would take to leave their flat and walk down three flights of stairs. There was no movement from within the lobby.

Oliver hurried out onto the street. He didn't want to run as he didn't want to draw attention to himself. But he moved with more than a degree of urgency. To any resident or bystander his actions were indicative of someone being late, not someone surveilling a target.

Once Oliver reached the street he glanced in both directions. Firstly, in the most logical direction, towards the local shops, then a brief glance in the other direction, before hastily walking towards the shops.

This he deduced, having considered that Sullivan was out of shape, and only leaving his flat to visit the shops for essentials, and maybe to get a minute amount of fresh air and exercise in the process, probably on his doctor's recommendation.

"Coz we don't want this fucker dropping dead on us, do we?" Oliver thought as he hastened his way to the shops, *"not when we're paying for his fucking fags, anyway."*

Oliver was referring to the fact that as Sullivan was in the halfway hostel after almost a year it was most likely because he had so far failed to secure any employment. As a result, he was relying on benefits and government hand-outs in addition to what was undoubtedly hugely subsidised, if not free, accommodation.

As Oliver made his way to the shops he recounted his readings about crime and punishment: That there is no deterrent factor regarding imprisonment. The re-offending rate amongst released prisoners was too high to believe that any form of rehabilitation had taken place. It had been proved that offenders didn't see prison as a punishment. Some admitted to offending just to get a free lifestyle for a duration. This was most prevalent around Christmas. It was seen as a win-win situation for the criminal; if they got away with the offence, they could go on to further offend. If they got caught, then there was also a positive outcome of a cost and hassle-free existence for the duration of their sentence. Even sentencing was not designed to be a punishment, not with judges avoiding handing out custodial sentences in favour of community orders and suspended sentences. In many cases, it was supposed that the convict would inwardly want to shake the judge's hand.

Oliver crossed the road as he rounded the last corner so as to be on the wrong side of the road to the shops. He didn't want to run the risk of passing Sullivan on the street and for him to have any suspicion raised should he recognise Oliver as being the man he passed in the doorway the previous evening. There was no reason why that should raise suspicion. Oliver expected that the occupancy of the block was fairly transient, with residents being there only for a short time before settling themselves elsewhere. Oliver was, however, grateful that Sullivan was perhaps the exception to this rule.

As Oliver cleared the corner he now had a view along the whole length of the parade of shops. The parade consisted of maybe a dozen or so shops. But only a few were still open at this time of the evening; there was a fish and chip shop with a steamed-up front window, beyond that was an Indian restaurant, called, rather originally, The Taj Mahal. There was also a Chinese takeaway and a mini-supermarket which had late opening hours.

He had not seen Sullivan on his approach. He was hoping he was inside one of these shops. He was frustrated with himself for letting himself get distracted earlier. "You fucking idiot," he called himself aloud. He checked his watch again. He was still within the rough time-frame of Sullivan's outing the previous evening. Oliver sat on a low garden wall in front of one the houses opposite. He waited.

Oliver allowed himself a moment to forgive himself. It wasn't the end of the world if he had missed Sullivan. He was prepared to stay beyond the next day anyway. Worst case scenario would be to stay another day beyond that. The way Oliver saw it, was that one occasion of leaving the flat of an evening didn't prove anything, twice was merely a coincidence, but based on three times this *could* be considered a habit, and potentially could be relied upon. He started to relax and breathe a little easier.

He was only there for a minute or so when he saw a figure he believed to be Sullivan walk out of the mini-supermarket. On this occasion he had apparently bought more than just cigarettes, as he was carrying a bag. Having cleared the shop doorway Sullivan paused. He opened the packet of cigarettes he had just bought, removed the cellophane and dropped it on the ground, despite standing immediately next to a waste bin. This just underlined the contempt that Oliver had for this man, that fourteen years of incarceration, and so-called rehabilitation, had achieved absolutely nothing in preparing this man for reintegration into a civilised society. There was a bright flash as the lighter sparked to life, then a plume of smoke escaped above Sullivan. He then set off in the direction of home.

Oliver maintained his position in order to allow Sullivan to walk across in front of him and get sufficiently ahead of him. All Oliver needed to do was keep Sullivan in sight, to ensure he went home after his little excursion. Today was all about routines and timings.

Once Sullivan was a sufficient distance ahead of him Oliver set off. He kept his distance. He found he was having to walk very slowly to maintain a constant distance behind Sullivan.

Oliver was paying particular attention to Sullivan's stature, his posture and the way he walked. For a man in his forties, he didn't appear to be in particularly good health.

As they walked, Oliver realised that in order to get that far ahead of him, despite his slow pace, Sullivan had to have left home mere moments into Oliver's distraction; when he was too focused on that fateful night as opposed to the task at hand.

That fateful night. Oliver again felt himself getting consumed by memories and hatred. To such an extent, that upon realisation he looked up to find he had almost halved the distance between him and Sullivan. He stopped and moved over into the shadows to allow Sullivan to regain his original lead.

Sullivan then turned the last corner into Allingham Road. As he turned, Oliver was sure he saw Sullivan look back at him. He wasn't one hundred percent sure, but sure enough to feel uncomfortable about it. Was Sullivan aware he was being followed? He wasn't about to take a chance and disappeared into the first driveway he passed.

Oliver crouched down behind the boundary fence, but of all the driveways he could have chosen, he chose one that had a gravel drive, one that drew enough attention to him when he darted across it.

From where he hid behind the fence, Oliver could hear footsteps coming along the pavement. They passed in front of him, getting louder as they did. Then they stopped. Oliver didn't dare emerge from where he was hidden. He then heard the same sound of shoes on gravel as he had just caused. Someone was on the driveway. From the shadows, Oliver could now see a figure on the driveway. A figure silhouetted by the streetlight across the road. Oliver was sure it was Sullivan. The silhouette took a long draw on a cigarette. The glow lighting up the face before being consumed by smoke. It *was* Sullivan. He turned to look in all directions. Once satisfied, he walked off the drive, again crunching on the loose gravel.

Oliver maintained his position. There was no way he was going to risk coming out to be ambushed by Sullivan.

When Oliver did eventually come out from behind the fence, he left in the direction of the shops. He ran the long way around, to approach Sullivan's block from the other direction. His heart was pounding as he tried to control his breathing.

He approached Sullivan's building, walked the left-hand side passage, passing the dumpsters. He then looked up to see lights on in Sullivan's flat. It looked like he did just come straight home after coming back to check for Oliver.

Although Oliver felt disappointed for allowing himself to be so easily distracted, a distraction which nearly resulted in Sullivan realising he was being followed, he was happy with the result of the evening.

With that, Oliver headed back to the B&B.

Chapter Twenty-One

"Sir, I have the audits you requested," the Detective Sergeant in charge of the investigation into Oliver's complaint said as he set down some papers on his supervisor's desk.

The Detective Sergeant in question, Lucas Simmonds, worked within the police in a department known as Professional Standards. This is an internal department, much like the Internal Affairs referenced in many American cop shows. The police *Police*, who are looking inwards at the integrity and professionalism of its officers, and who investigate them in such circumstances as when Oliver's complaint was upheld.

"Anything of interest?" the Detective Inspector replied, without even giving Simmonds the courtesy of looking at him when he was addressed.

"Yeah, I think you're gonna want to see this, and sooner rather than later," Simmonds anxiously replied.

"Why's that?" was how the DI responded, trying to dismiss the urgency his underling approached him with.

"This goes a lot deeper than Bennett just being heavy handed with a suspect," he paused, "a *lot* deeper."

This finally got the full attention of the DI. He stopped what he was doing and sat back in his chair. He laced his fingers behind his head and sat there looking smugly arrogant, as if defying Simmonds to make good on his previous remark.

"Well, sir," Simmonds began, "as you know we always run checks on what database searches officers under investigation have been conducting to see if there is any other impropriety. Y'know, the usual, have they been running checks on their partners, ex-partner's new partner et cetera. Well, what we've found on Bennett goes far beyond that. Far beyond anything I've *ever* seen."

Simmonds certainly now had his Inspector's full attention.

"Go on," he said, his own voice now matching the urgency of his Sergeant.

"Well, there's something that has been grossly overlooked when it comes to PC Bennett, sir." Simmonds paused to take a breath. "When he was a boy his mother was murdered."

The DI sat forward in his chair. He rested his elbows on the desk and clasped his fingers together, resting his chin on his hands. He stared intently, anxiously awaiting to hear what Simmonds had to say.

"His mother's killer, a Marc Sullivan, was caught and convicted, he served fourteen years of a life sentence and was released last year. The release was a matter of public record, but no personal details were released. PC Bennett was only five years old when this happened. He's been in and out of counselling ever since."

"How did we not know about this on his application?" the DI enquired.

"Well, we did, but these days so many applicants flag as having been in counselling or therapy, or having been on prescribed medication for mental health issues, that we don't probe beneath the obvious."

"And what about the mother?" the DI asked.

"Well, she was never included on the application as being a relative, I mean, why would she, she was dead. And Oliver's name didn't raise any flags."

"So, what has he found out about his mother's killer?"

"I don't know what he's found out, but *I* was able to find out Sullivan's release date and the bail hostel he was released to. But that was all last year. I don't know if it's current or not."

"Okay," the DI interjected, "first things first. Safeguarding, we need to make sure this Sullivan guy is okay. You're gonna have to have the local Force pay him a visit and do a welfare check."

"Okay," Simmonds said as he was taking a note of the DI's instructions.

"But," the DI added, "don't make him aware of the situation. We don't want to cause a panic, or give him a reason to start tooling himself up. Also, we're gonna need to speak to Bennett about this too. Best pop round to see him, get him in, so we can put this to him."

Once Simmonds had finished scribbling down his plan of action, he nodded his acknowledgement and left his Inspector's office.

Chapter Twenty-Two

Oliver decided to allow the dust to settle on the previous efforts to determine Sullivan's routines. As a result, he didn't go near his flat or the shops local to him at all the following day. It resulted in a wasted day, and unnecessary expense, but it was a very necessary evil. Oliver couldn't afford to raise Sullivan's suspicions.

He did, however, make good use of his time. He spent the day deciding how to make best use of the intelligence he had gathered on Sullivan's routine, and how best to monopolise it. Oliver also spent a great deal of time sitting in a café across town scrutinising the classified section of the local newspapers. He was looking for something very specific, something ideally suited to his needs.

With one paper open he dragged the forefinger of his left hand down the page whilst using his right hand to take a sip from his nearly cold coffee. It was then he saw exactly what he was looking for. In his excitement, the coffee cup was returning to the table more exuberantly than he had planned. The resulting noise caught the attention of everyone still in the café at just after eleven o'clock in the morning. Oliver gave a brief glance around, to find all eyes on him. He could see an old boy by the door had already drawn his own conclusions and was seen to be muttering something under his breath as he disapprovingly shook his head. The *mums who lunch* group also gave a disapproving look, which was more out of concern that Oliver's outburst would upset their sleeping babies. Finally, Oliver looked over at the serving counter and gave an apologetic head tilt, as well as mouthing the word 'sorry' to the server behind the counter. Peace resumed.

Oliver kept his finger on the classified article that had excited him so much. He took his phone from his pocket and started to dial the number from the article. He looked around, the last thing he wanted to do was to draw further attention to himself following what had just happened. When questioned, people have a greater recollection of details when their attention is on someone. This phone call could be a recalled detail if people's attention was on him. Oliver stood from his table.

"I'll be right back," he said to the server behind the counter. She was aware that Oliver had yet to pay his tab. She looked at him, then looked at the table. She could see his coat on the back of his chair. She then reasoned that he was not in the process of doing a runner and not paying his tab. She went back to her previous task. Oliver slipped outside.

It was cold outside, too cold to be outside without a coat. But Oliver knew it would only be a short call. He pressed *send* on the number he had already dialled. The phone rang, it was answered. Oliver spoke, "I'm ringing about the article in the paper, has it been sold yet?"

After the reply, Oliver continued, "That's great, it's just what I'm looking for. The article says it's in excellent overall condition, is that right?" Oliver was silent as his question was answered in detail which met Oliver's approval.

"That's great," Oliver replied. "I'll definitely take it, if it's as you say. Two things though; I don't know the area very well, so how far are you from the town centre? And secondly, I won't be able to get to you until next week." Oliver paused to allow a reply, when that was concluded he continued, "Oh, obviously, yeah, if you have someone else interested in the meantime then go with them, otherwise I'll have it, cash okay?"

After another short pause whilst Oliver was given some more information. "Okay, thanks for that, I'll be in contact next week then, can you message me on this number if it sells though?"

Oliver then ended the call and went back inside. It was only once he was back inside that he realised how cold he was. He shuddered with the cold as he went back to his table.

"Can I have another coffee please?" he asked of the server as he passed her.

The last thing Oliver needed was another cup of coffee, he was already feeling the caffeine buzz from the previous two, but this one was more to warm him up than wake him up.

The third coffee turned breakfast into lunch and Oliver found himself passing more time than he had expected at the café. Today, he wasn't in any hurry. He had already achieved more than he had planned for. He knew he would be out in the cold later, so he was allowing himself to enjoy the warmth of his surroundings now. Unfortunately, he wasn't able to partake of his hobby of people-watching, as the difference in temperatures and the humidity in the café meant that the front windows were steamed up, making the viewing of passers-by almost impossible.

oOo

Later that evening Oliver took up position once more. Same time, same vantage point. The purpose this time was to prove the habit. Once didn't count, twice could be seen as a coincidence, but three times was a deliberate act, and could be seen as a pattern, or a habit. However, on this occasion. Oliver felt as if he couldn't run the risk of being discovered as with his previous effort. All he needed to ascertain was that Sullivan left his flat at approximately the same time, and was out for approximately the same duration. He could determine that from outside his home address, just by observing the front door. Oliver didn't need to know where Sullivan went, he didn't need to follow him this time.

Oliver had taken up position in the far-right corner of the rear grounds as he had done previously. From there he could clearly see the windows of Sullivan's flat, as well as along the side passage that led to the front door. Oliver had also purchased a cheap pair of binoculars from an army surplus shop that afternoon. They were a military spec pair, with slotted covers for the front lenses to minimise any reflection. So, from his vantage point, and using the binoculars he was able to see in enough detail that it was Sullivan leaving and returning.

So as not to be bamboozled, should Sullivan make an unexpectedly early departure, Oliver took up position in good time. The binoculars weren't the only item Oliver bought from the army surplus shop, another item was a hooded poncho. He was already wearing it. It was long enough to sit on, and completely encapsulate him in waterproof and weatherproof olive-green nylon. Until now, he had been dressed in what he had considered appropriate for the weather, but it was the wind-chill he hadn't been prepared for. Now, however, he felt he could maintain this position, dependent only on food and rest. Oliver was thankful, though, that this wouldn't be required, at least not this evening. He hoped this wouldn't be a prolonged observation.

Oliver would frequently check the windows of Sullivan's flat. The lights in the larger of the two windows, which he presumed was the living room, were on, and had been since he first arrived. The window next to it was smaller, and the light in this room went on and off several times. The smaller of the two windows, he concluded, must be the bedroom. This was purely supposition, and an educated guess. Given the purpose of these flats, he felt they must be one-bedroom flats, most likely consisting of a combined living room and kitchenette, one bedroom and a bathroom.

The light then came on again in the assumed bedroom. It was on only for about a minute before being turned off again. Then the living room light turned off for the first time since Oliver had arrived. He was sure this was Sullivan in preparation to go out. Oliver checked his watch. He was happy that this time was consistent with the other times he had observed. Sullivan's flat was now in darkness. Oliver trained the binoculars on the side passage towards the front door. He counted since seeing the lights in Sullivan's flat go dark.

"One Mississippi, two Mississippi, three Mississippi…" he counted. Oliver had rehearsed and realised that counting Mississippi's was more accurate than counting *one one-thousand, two one-thousand, three one-thousand* et cetera.

Sullivan took to the count of thirty-six Mississippi's from the moment the lights went out, having descended three flights of stairs, to appearing outside of the front door. Oliver only had the briefest of glimpses of Sullivan in profile before he turned his back towards him. This in itself was reassuring for Oliver. He felt this showed a calm and relaxed Sullivan, one who had not been unduly spooked by the mishap of two evenings ago. There was no sign of a cautious glance down the side passage, no looking over his shoulder. For Oliver, this was ideal. He had hoped that Sullivan wouldn't have thought anything of the other night and not read anything into it, and from the looks of this, he hadn't.

Once Sullivan was out of sight, Oliver checked his watch again. He started the stopwatch, he also started waiting, again.

To occupy himself during the interim, Oliver imagined the route he had taken on the previous occasion. He imagined walking the streets in real time. Keeping a constant distance from his target, losing him momentarily at corners, then rushing up to regain line of sight.

Oliver viewed his stopwatch intermittently. When he did, he ducked his head down inside the poncho so as not to illuminate himself in any way. From the time shown, he expected Sullivan to be at the turnaround point now, the shops. Oliver pictured himself watching him from across the street as he had done previously. He then reset himself, binoculars in both hands, eyes intent on the side passage. He waited.

A figure came into view along the side passage. Oliver brought the binoculars up to view the figure through them. It wasn't Sullivan. He heard the faintest buzz, over the silence that surrounded him. This person must be visiting someone in the block.

A few seconds passed, then there was a second buzz. Oliver hadn't seen anyone else coming or going. He assumed it must be the same person still waiting to be let in, hidden within the alcove.

"Oh, take a fucking hint," Oliver muttered to himself, "look you're not being let in, now fuck off!"

Then there was a loud thud, and Oliver could see the same figure walking away towards the street showing apparent disapproval at not being admitted into the building.

Oliver was itching to take another look at his stopwatch, he felt Sullivan's return must now be imminent. But the process of bringing his limbs and head inside the poncho was a lengthy one, he didn't want to miss Sullivan's actual return. So, he waited.

He didn't have to wait long. After what must've been less than a minute after the disgruntled visitor had left, Sullivan returned. Oliver viewed him through the binoculars. He was puffing away on a cigarette, a plume of smoke rising above him as he walked along the side passage. He had a bag of shopping in each hand. His head was bowed, his gaze appeared to be on the ground.

As Sullivan stepped up the single step into the alcove to the front door, he tripped. He instinctively dropped a shopping bag in an attempt to catch himself against the wall.

Oliver had to bite his bottom lip to prevent himself from sniggering, or having any audible reaction. Sullivan was completely out of sight in the alcove. As a result, Oliver had no idea when to start counting Mississippi's to mark Sullivan's return to his flat, his gaze switching intermittently between the side passage and the top floor flat's windows. Oliver knew he daren't glance at his watch until he knew Sullivan's whereabouts. He was starting to feel uncomfortable about the situation. The last he had seen of Sullivan was him tripping into the alcove. Was he injured? For a moment, Oliver had a bout of conscience when he thought of Sullivan. He could be hurt. But before Oliver could entertain this notion any further, the living room light came on in Sullivan's flat, shortly followed briefly by the bedroom light. Sullivan was alive at least, Oliver thought. Unknown if he was injured. Oliver stopped the stopwatch without looking at it.

Oliver thought it best to give Sullivan a minute or two to settle in before leaving himself. In this time, he began stripping off and packing up his poncho. He felt surprisingly warm considering the climate. Once it was packed away, he checked the lights in the flat, they were still on, no visible signs of Sullivan, but he appeared never to go out and leave the lights on. Oliver felt it was safe to emerge from his hiding place.

He kept to the perimeter tree line as he approached the side passage. Once in the passage, he saw that something had been spilled in the alcove, a liquid. It wasn't milk, that was all Oliver was able to deduce. He felt this most likely happened when Sullivan dropped his shopping to give himself a free hand to cushion his fall. Another thing Oliver noticed was that a lower pane of glass had been cracked since he was last there. He paused for a moment to look at it, it was on the pane adjacent to the front door, below the letterbox. Had Sullivan caused this when he fell? If so, it was a substantial impact as this was safety glass. Then after a moment, he remembered the disgruntled visitor, the one who left without being admitted. Did he cause this? It was about the right height from the ground to be caused by a kick. In the available light, and the time he had, Oliver found it impossible to draw any conclusion. He knew he had to leave. However it was caused, it wouldn't change what was going to happen next.

Chapter Twenty-Three

Paul Bennett hadn't long been up when he heard the doorbell ring, followed immediately by an impatient knocking. Before leaving the kitchen, he glanced at the clock on the wall, it said 7:52 a.m., the clock on the cooker said the same when Paul felt he needed a second opinion. He wasn't expecting any deliveries or post, so was sceptical when he approached the door. Through the glazed panels, he could see silhouetted in the early morning light two figures standing on the doorstep. He opened the door to them.

"Good morning, I am Detective Sergeant Lucas Simmonds, and this is Detective Constable Walker, does an Oliver Bennett live here?"

Paul Bennett took a moment to glance at both of the men standing before him. Although he knew he had nothing to hide, he felt angered by this early morning interruption.

"Yes, he does," Bennett replied, intentionally keeping his answers limited to the absolute bare minimum.

"Is he home?" DS Simmonds asked.

"No, he's not," Bennett replied.

"Is he going to be home today?" Simmonds continued with his questions. Bennett just shrugged his shoulders.

"Mr Bennett," Simmonds said, standing tall, trying to add an air of authority to the moment. "Do you know where your son is right now?"

Paul Bennett leaned against the doorframe and folded his arms. He felt this may appear insolent to his interrogator, and if so, it was a case of mission accomplished.

"No, Sergeant," he paused and shook his head, "I don't know where my son is."

"Mister Bennett, we do have some questions we'd like to ask you about your son. May we come in?"

Bennett pushed himself away from the door frame and stepped aside. He implied an invitation to his visitors. First Simmonds, then Walker entered the house. They stopped in the hallway until Bennett had shut the front door and walked past them to lead them into the kitchen.

As Simmonds entered the kitchen he could smell coffee, he looked around and saw a filter machine on the counter with a full pot that had just been made.

Bennett took a seat at the breakfast bar. This had been his previously intended seat as there was a steaming mug of coffee already placed there. The one that he was about to enjoy before the knock at the door. He beckoned the two Detectives to sit at the dining table beyond the breakfast bar. Once everyone was seated, Simmonds continued his questioning.

"When did you last see your son, Mister Bennett?" He asked.

"I… saw… him," Bennett paused for a moment to count back the days accurately before responding, "Tuesday morning."

"Tuesday morning?" Walker repeated back to confirm the answer. Bennett merely nodded. "Did he say where he was going?"

"He didn't say, and I didn't ask," Bennett said.

"Did you know he is on suspension from work?" Simmonds added.

"Yep," Bennett replied, "he mentioned that to me on Monday evening."

"What did he tell you about *why* he was on suspension?" Walker added.

"He mentioned it, and we discussed it, some bullshit about assaulting some scumbag who rips off old people," Bennett replied. At this reply, he could see Walker feverishly scribbling some notes in his notepad.

"Scumbag, eh?" Simmonds asked, "your word or his?"

"Whose?" Bennett asked.

"Your son's," Simmonds clarified.

"Seriously? You're asking me if someone who rips off old folks isn't a scumbag?" Simmonds could see that Bennett was becoming agitated at that question. Agitation would cause him to become defensive, and defensive would not get them anywhere. He knew he had to take the conversation in a different direction to get Bennett back on-side.

"Mister Bennett," Simmonds paused to ensure his next questions was phrased accurately to ensure the best response, "does the name Marc Sullivan mean anything to you?"

The hand that Bennett was resting his chin on came crashing down on the breakfast bar. More by luck than judgment it narrowly missed the coffee mug. He turned his head to look out of the window. He could clearly be seen to mutter, "For fuck's sake!"

"Are you kidding me?" he replied. "Are you having a fucking laugh? You come into my home and ask me if I know the name of the man who killed my wife? Are you for fucking real?"

Simmonds felt suitably embarrassed at his gross lack of professional judgment. Walker felt equally embarrassed and shocked by what should've been an expected reaction from Bennett.

Both Simmonds and Walker had been working in the Professional Standards Department for some time. During that time, their liaisons and interactions had predominantly been dealings with police officers. It would appear they had lost their skills when it came to dealing with *real* people, members of the public.

Bennett realised the element of control and leadership in this discussion had shifted significantly since the last comment. He had a day ahead planned and needed to expedite the conversation, if for no other reason than to rid himself of the two imbeciles sitting before him.

"Look, Detective, stop beating around the bush, just tell me why you felt the need to come banging on my front door at seven fifty-two in the fucking morning?"

This in itself highlighted that Bennett wasn't dealing with a MENSA day trip, as they both looked at their watches in perfect unison. Bennett pictured them both having matching Mickey Mouse watches. After what seemed a painfully long time, Simmonds was the first to speak.

"Mister Bennett, we believe that your son has been trying to locate Sullivan." Simmonds paused to allow himself to view Bennett's reaction to this revelation.

When none came, he felt compelled to continue. "It appears he has been using police databases to obtain information as to where Sullivan was housed after his release."

"Housed? Do you mean we're still paying for this fucker?" Bennett exclaimed.

"That's irrelevant at this time, Mister Bennett. Unauthorised access of police databases is a serious offence. We need to speak to your son in order to establish what he knows, and his intentions. Now obviously we know all about Sullivan and your family, and that will be taken into consideration when we look to resolve this situation."

"Well, obviously, you didn't know everything, I mean, I'm guessing none of this flagged up when Ollie applied for the job in the first place. I bet nothing flagged up on Ollie when he applied, did it?" Bennett started to get agitated again.

"I have to say that is true, Mister Bennett, nothing was raised when your son made his initial application. This was because he was too young at the time to play an active part in the Sullivan case, and your name as his next of kin wasn't linked either."

"And *had* it flagged up?" Bennett asked, putting Simmonds on the spot.

"Then, chances are, his application would've been rejected on that basis alone," Simmonds replied.

"So, what you're essentially saying is," Bennett paused, "you've given him the means to come face-to-face with the man who murdered his mother. And yet, no doubt, you'll hold him responsible for what happens next. Essentially, you've given a child a loaded gun, and then blame him when he shoots someone!"

Both Simmonds and Walker could see the anger and upset building in Bennett's face.

"But it's not going to be like that, is it? Otherwise, he wouldn't already be on suspension, and you wouldn't be here – no doubt looking to arrest him. Well, he's not here, I don't know where he is. And to tell you the truth, I wouldn't tell you *even* if I did. There's no way in hell I'm gonna hand him over to be hung out to dry by you lot. Blaming him for your fuck ups! What happens, happens, on *your* heads, be it!"

Both Simmonds and Walker appeared to shrink in their chairs. Both of them realised that Bennett had a valid point. There was no way that had the full facts about Oliver's past been known, would he have ever been offered the role of Constable. Now, as a result, he had been given access to all the information he would need in order to locate his mother's killer.

"I think we're done here," Simmonds said. His voice came out in a pitch a little higher than normal. He was feeling emotional at the gravity of the situation, and the likelihood of an unpleasant outcome.

"We may very well make further calls in order to try to speak to your son," he added. He knew this was a futile comment. He knew full well that the moment he and Walker left the house that Bennett would be straight on the phone to his son. Telling him that the police have been to the house looking for him, looking to speak to him for the unauthorised accessing of police databases.

The penny suddenly dropped for Bennett. Oliver had been away all week. Initially, Bennett thought he was just having some time away after the revelation of the suspension. But now, given this visit, maybe Oliver was there now, maybe he was actually tracking down Sullivan.

'*Ohmigod!*' he thought.

"We'll be off now," Simmonds said, bringing Bennett back to the moment.

"Okay," Bennett replied. He was out of his seat and back towards the front door before Simmonds and Walker had even finished standing up.

As they walked past him, and out of the front door, Simmonds said to Bennett. "Will you give us a call when you hear from him?"

"Of course, I will," Bennett replied.

Both knew each other's comment was a complete waste of time but said merely to entertain the other.

Once the door was closed, Bennett returned to the kitchen. He resumed his seat at the breakfast bar. He picked up his coffee. His hand was shaking as he lifted the mug to his mouth. He didn't know what to think, or how to feel.

So many thoughts then swamped his mind; he'd already lost his wife to Sullivan, did he now stand a chance of losing his son to him too? He wanted justice for his wife's death, but surely this wasn't the way, was it?

He was torn about what he wanted to happen, but the overriding factor was that he didn't want to lose his son. It appeared every outcome had him lose his son, either to Sullivan or to the police.

It took some time for Bennett to process all he had been told by the police. What he had told them was true, they *did* have an overwhelming responsibility for the situation. They had in fact created this situation, by allowing Oliver access to the databases to indulge his fantasies. Had they not done so, that's all they would have remained as, fantasies.

Bennett himself had many fantasies over the years, exacerbated by Oliver's ongoing hardship at dealing with the experience. He had imagined himself engaging with Sullivan one-on-one, with his timeless face from the courtroom being beaten to a bloody pulp. Whilst in others, seeing him face the full sentence of the now abolished law. Or utilising some of the awful techniques that Oliver had himself described from his macabre studies of medieval torture and punishment.

Then for the second time that morning, Bennett had another revelation. Was this morbid fascination merely pre-planning, waiting for this opportunity before him to take place? Were the karate lessons merely an attempt to make him combat-ready, on the off-chance he and Sullivan would one day meet?

Was joining the police, and undergoing all the legislative and procedural training, merely a means to an end to gain access to the information he so desperately needed? To provide the final piece of the puzzle?

Was *everything* in Oliver's life a means to an end to gain him the skills, knowledge and then the information he required, to put him face-to-face with Sullivan?

Chapter Twenty-Four

Oliver was in the shower when his phone rang. But when he came out he found he had a voicemail message and a text message. He read the message before listening to the voicemail. The message read:

Ollie, the police were here this morning, they want to speak to you about accessing information about Sullivan. Is that where you are now? Do what you feel is right, but be careful...

"Bollocks!" Oliver exclaimed at seeing the message. Until now he thought he had the luxury of time on his side. He didn't realise his complaint would generate such scrutiny about his other activities. It wasn't going to change the outcome, however, just expedite the schedule.

After he was dried off and dressed. He picked up his phone again. He firstly listened to the voicemail his father had left him. Then he accessed the list of the most recent numbers dialled, selected one and hit send. After a few rings, the call was answered.

"Hello." He paused as he listened to the reply. "I phoned the other day, is it still available?" after another pause. "Great! Slight change of plan, I need it sooner than expected, can I pick it up today at some point?"

There was another pause as Oliver listened to what was being said to him. "Fab, that'll do nicely, I'll see you then, cash in hand. Are you able to text me the address as I don't have the means to write anything down right now? Cheers."

The call ended, and moments later his phone beeped signifying a text message had been received. Good to his word, the text gave the full address that Oliver needed to attend. The address came through as a hyperlink, so when Oliver clicked on it, it came up in the phone's navigation app and showed him a pedestrian route to get there. It was some distance across town, but it was still early morning, and Oliver had all morning to get there.

oOo

"It's perfect," Oliver said as he was shown around what he had gone to view, "I'll take it."

Whilst the seller went off to get the necessary paperwork, Oliver was left to have a look round his new acquisition on his own. He had viewed quite a few classified articles the morning he spent in the café, several came close, but only this one had met all of his needs.

In itself it was nothing remarkable, after all it was only a Ford Transit van. The only exceptional feature was the fact that it was a hi-top, short wheelbase version and came with roof bars and a towing hook. He had just come back from taking it for a test-drive. All that remained was to hand over the cash and complete a minimal amount of paperwork.

Due to the age and condition of the vehicle, Oliver was only required to hand over £500 for the van. He didn't even haggle over the price even though the advertisement did say *ONO,* or near offer.

When the seller returned to where he had left Oliver with the van, he found Oliver in the process of testing the sliding side door. He was opening and closing it, appearing to use one hand then the other, before seeing Oliver jump into the back and see how tall he could actually stand up within it. With it being the hi-top version, Oliver was able to stand up fully without the need to stoop or risk banging his head on the roof. When Oliver saw the seller, he jumped down out of the van and joined the seller on the roadside.

Although Oliver owned a car he had never spent any time scrutinising the vehicle registration document. This was because he was given the VW for his birthday, and his father had taken care of all the necessary paperwork.

The seller was thankfully much more proficient in completing the registration certificate for this sale. He used the bed of the back of the van as an improvised desk. He started to complete the details required for the new registered keeper. He asked the questions he needed to ask in order to complete that section of the document.

"Name and address?" he asked.

"Marc with a 'C', Sullivan, double 'L'. Address is Flat 15, 46 Allingham Road," Oliver replied. He was also asked for a date of birth, which he was able to provide. This again was accurate information which Oliver had obtained from a police database.

With the form complete, cash handed over and counted twice, and a receipt issued for the transaction, the deal was done. Following sealing the deal with a firm handshake, Oliver was left on the roadside with his new acquisition.

He looked at his watch. He concluded it was time for lunch. He climbed up into the cab of his new vehicle. All he had to do now was drive sensibly, and park considerately, unlike most Transit drivers he thought, and *not* draw any attention to himself. As he started the engine, he glanced at the fuel gauge. It was just under half full. This would probably be plenty for what he needed, but he thought it best to stick twenty quid in there, just in case.

oOo

As per the last few days, lunch consisted of a café meal. However, this time, Oliver found a 'greasy spoon' truck stop just outside of town. It had the convenience of having petrol pumps. It wasn't a main chain service station, so it had the added benefit of not having any CCTV.

Oliver sat down and enjoyed an all-day breakfast. Next to his plate he had a notepad. On it was a list of items he still needed to procure. But also, he had written down items that he had already obtained and that he had brought with him from home. As he ate, he thought, and as he thought so things would be added to the list.

As with the previous days he had been away from home, the days hadn't been particularly busy. But today, the call from his father had instilled a certain degree of urgency in Oliver. That call had led to him to purchase the van earlier than expected and bring his schedule forward. It was now a Thursday. This evening would have a better chance of having Sullivan follow his weekday evening routine than tomorrow, being a Friday. On a Friday there was a greater chance of him breaking this routine to enjoy some frivolities, or worse still, have company.

Then Oliver gave consideration to the fact that being on the dole does have certain similarities to working shifts. For Oliver, a Friday is rarely a Friday in the traditional sense. It doesn't necessarily mark the end of the working week. Neither does it for someone on the dole. You can't have an end to the working week if you don't work, he thought. The fact that tomorrow was a Friday may just be a red herring.

Every time that Oliver thought the list was nearing completion, another item would occur to him that would require adding. Eventually, he concluded that he had covered all eventualities, and that the list was more or less complete. *More or less* in respect that further items could be added *should* the need arise. Once completed thus far, he began marking with an asterisk all of the items that he had so far obtained. He then decided where best to obtain the outstanding items. Luckily for him, they were all general hardware, and for those, he recalled passing a retail park prior to arriving at the café.

Having finished his lunch and his list, and having settled his bill, Oliver set out to obtain everything he felt he would now need.

Chapter Twenty-Five

"Sir," DS Simmonds said as he knocked on the open glass door to his Inspector's office.

His Inspector was sitting in his chair with his back turned to the door when the knock was heard. He spun around to see who it was. He had his mobile phone to his ear and was engaged in a conversation. He turned to face Simmonds and indicated; firstly, that he was on the phone by pointing to the less than conspicuous handset pressed against his face, and secondly, he held up his free hand with a single finger extended, indicating that the remainder of the call would be brief, and that Simmonds could or should wait. Once he got a nodded response from Simmonds, the Inspector rotated his chair back the way it had been prior to the intrusion and concluded the call in an identical posture that Simmonds had first found him.

A few moments later the call was ended. The Inspector lowered the handset from his head. Simmonds could hear a few words being muttered but couldn't deduce what they were. Then the Inspector rotated his chair, so he was again facing Simmonds.

"Yes, Lucas," he paused to take a breath, "what can I do for you?"

"Sir, with regards to the Bennett investigation." He paused to allow his Inspector to recall the details previously discussed. When he got the desired response, he continued, "We've had a response from the Force that was trying to make contact with Marc Sullivan."

It was then that the Inspector was no longer able to fake that he knew what Simmonds was talking about. He had to oversee and review numerous cases, so as a result sometimes the details of any specific one would escape him. Finally admitting defeat, he had to make his confession to his Sergeant.

"Lucas, you're gonna have to rewind it a bit, sorry, I'm a little lost at the mo', who's Sullivan?"

Realising that he was now going to have to recap the investigation in order to bring the Inspector up to speed, Simmonds stepped forward into the office from the doorway and leant himself on the back of a chair opposite the Inspector.

"Well, sir," Simmonds began, "we are currently investigating one of our officers for an alleged assault during arrest. Since then we have also discovered that he has possibly been using police databases to ascertain the whereabouts of the man who killed his mother some fourteen plus years ago, and who has been released in the last year."

"Okay," replied the Inspector, "and what's your update?"

"Well, we've had the local police try to make contact with Marc Sullivan, the released killer, to a – confirm his whereabouts, b – determine his welfare, and c – give consideration to warning him that someone may be targeting him, but obviously not giving any specific details as to who. Well, we've heard back from the local Force, they've supposedly made repeated attempts to locate Sullivan at his home address, and so far, there's been no answer. They're looking to close their report on this, unless they get an Inspector's authority to keep it open and make further attempts."

There was a silence in the Inspector's office as he considered the information just laid before him. As with everything in the police, every decision was a balancing act.

Decisions had to be justified and be explainable should they ever be scrutinised. Decisions had to be made, and conclusions reached using what was known as the National Decision Making (NDM) model. Officers were no longer able to make decisions based on sound judgment and common sense. They had to use this model, and document their rationale in reaching the decisions they did. It was said, if it wasn't written down, it didn't happen. So, this led to a culture of over documenting and arse-covering. The model was designed to allow for sound judgment, but it only had the effect of everyone erring on the side of caution, scared that if a decision was flawed then they would be criticised.

As a result, resources were often deployed for a greater duration than necessary because supervising officers were often scared to make a decision that went against any decision made previously.

The Inspector had a decision in front of him, one, like so many others that wouldn't have a direct bearing on him, but one that could come back to bite him should it go pear-shaped.

The silence was broken by the Inspector. "We're gonna need to speak to this Sullivan at the very least. Again, have them give consideration to advising him that someone may be targeting him. And feed anything back to me, okay?"

Simmonds nodded.

Once again, the Inspector simply nodded along with the previous suggestions, not taking a decisive stand at all. 'Have them give consideration' was what was considered a sloping shoulders approach to decision making. It is essentially putting the decision on a subordinate's shoulders, then holding them accountable should it go wrong. In this case, advising Sullivan that someone is possibly targeting him could have serious ramifications. He could arm himself if he feels an attack is imminent or descend into a pit of self-abuse. But should the officer *not* choose to advise him, and the attack takes place, then the police would be criticised for having such information and *not* warning the target, at which point the more senior officer could relinquish responsibility by cascading the responsibility downwards. In some cases, to officers no more experienced than Oliver.

Having received a suitable response from the Inspector, Simmonds thanked him and left the office. Following the Inspector's decision, he would now instruct Sullivan's local Force to make continued attempts to locate and speak to him, and 'give consideration' to making him aware that someone may be targeting him.

Chapter Twenty-Six

Oliver spent his afternoon selecting and purchasing all the items that weren't marked with an asterisk on his list. The list didn't contain a significant number of items, and most of those that were on the list were small. Oliver was able to collect those in a hand-held shopping basket. The only exception was a four-way folding ladder, the type that can be used as a straight ladder, an A frame, or variations in between. Once again, Oliver paid for these items in cash.

Back in the van, Oliver felt he needed to check one more thing before he could feel that everything was in readiness.

He had the who, Sullivan, he had the when, tomorrow night, he had the how, in the bags on the passenger seat beside him. He most definitely had the why; his mother. All that remained was the where, and Oliver knew exactly where.

He needed to know how long it would take to get to this location from Sullivan's home address and whether there were any roadworks or other variables that could cause delays along the way. Could he even remember exactly where *it* was along the road? These were all important factors that needed to be taken into consideration, and if necessary delay the 'when' until another time.

Oliver drove the route ensuring he strictly maintained the speed limits. He stopped at all amber lights, even if he felt he could, or should have gone through them. He was looking for a conservative time in order to reach the destination.

The destination, the exact same place where Oliver heard his mother's dying screams for help.

When Oliver arrived, he checked his watch. It had taken a little over forty-five minutes to drive the distance. This was in the early afternoon, before the evening rush hour. Oliver was also planning to drive this route again later that same evening at around eight o'clock, in order to give a real-time indicator for the journey. He didn't have to contend with a great deal of traffic and hadn't come up against any roadworks. He felt this would be a comparable time should he be driving the same route later that evening, and again the next day about the same time.

Oliver hadn't been back to this location since he was a child. He had no need to. However, he had researched the location when he was on restricted duties and with that, coupled with online satellite images, he was able to determine the lay-by in question that his mother had parked in on that evening, on that journey home, the journey that she would never complete.

When Oliver arrived, there was a scattering of commercial vehicles already parked up in the lay-by. He had passed a busier lay-by previously in order to reach this one. He felt the reason that one was busier was because it had a flower seller in it. As it was an unlit stretch of road, Oliver felt confident he wouldn't be there later, and that evening's recce should confirm that for him.

Once Oliver had parked, he realised that either he must approach the lay-by from the other direction, or that he needed to turn around. At present, the lay-by was on his offside. He would need it to be on his nearside, so as to have the van's sliding side door nearest to the woodland, and not facing into traffic as it was now.

With that noted and resolved in his mind, he then alighted from the van and went to the back and opened the rear doors

197

before having a brief rummage through the items he had recently purchased. He took one item from the bag; it was a folding pruning saw. He stripped it of all packaging and put the folded saw under his jacket..

From the photos from his mother's casefile, he was able to determine approximately where along the lay-by she had parked. He was then able to see a clear break in the foliage. Beside the gap, within a few feet was a red bin on a metal post intended for dog waste. This indicated two things to him; firstly, that this area was frequented by dog-walkers, but also, as the bin was overflowing, that the local council didn't visit all that often to empty it. It was also a useful marker for Oliver. Now knowing where to best pull up, he stepped through the gap.

Once on the other side a clear area opened up. In front of him was a raised mound of earth that ran along the edge of the lay-by as far as Oliver could see in both directions. He felt this was either here to prevent rainwater flooding the lay-by, or travellers being able to get beyond the lay-by to set up camp.

Beyond the mound of earth was a clearing as the single track branched off into many. The woodland was dense, though the canopy above them was sparse. As a result, there was a significant amount of natural light illuminating the area. Oliver had a clear view around him.

Oliver then spent the next couple of hours improving this area to further suit his future needs. He used the saw to trim the occasional branch here and there, both around the clearing but mainly to improve access through the foliage that separated the clearing from the lay-by. He knew that the next time he would be passing through that opening it would be dark, and in time, he would not be alone.

Oliver had to be careful when it came to improving access, he needed to make it easier for himself, but without making the entrance too obvious to anyone else. The last thing he wanted was to have a flurry of dog-walkers descend on the area. He needed to act quickly, to ideally have the job done this side of the weekend, when he felt this would be a more popular area.

When Oliver felt that all was in readiness, he sat down on the mound of earth and surveyed the area in front of him. He imagined how his mother had pulled up in the lay-by, much like he had done. How she then got out of the car to make a phone call only because as his father had told him, his mother was 'quite animated when she spoke on the phone'. It was said that she never stood still when she was talking, that she used to pace around, sometimes pacing up and down the hallway when at home, 'almost wearing a hole in the carpet' he'd say.

Oliver looked back towards the opening. Despite having improved the access, he couldn't see his van or the road beyond it because the foliage was so dense. He imagined where his mother had parked, where she had alighted from the car to make her 'animated' phone call, never straying too far from where he was strapped into the back seat.

In a moment Oliver had the recollection that she was making faces at him through the window and stroking the glass to reassure him. That was to be the last time he ever saw her.

At some point, she was either away from the side of the car or Oliver's attention was elsewhere, she was grabbed and dragged away from the lay-by.

Oliver recalled only hearing distant screams, nothing to suggest they were right beside the car. Sullivan may have covered her mouth until she was some distance from the road when he began his despicable act.

Despite the nature of the offence, and the victim being his mother, Oliver had read in excruciatingly painful detail exactly what had been stated in court that Sullivan had done to her.

As Oliver relived the accounts as he had read them, he stood up and walked the clearing, re-enacting the locations described as they occurred to him.

Oliver had seen photographs of where his mother's body had been left by Sullivan and found by police. He walked to this location, realising he was now standing on the exact spot where his mother had died. He looked back, towards the road, he was now out of sight of anyone not using the clearing. He reviewed the photos in his mind. She was found face down in the dirt. Leaves and mud covered her back, suggesting she had been rolled over at some point during the attack. Her clothes were torn, her dress was found to be pushed up above her waist. Her white knickers were muddied, bloodied and disturbed. Within her hands she held fistfuls of dirt, gripping down on it to help endure the pain she was suffering. Her face was turned to face back towards the road, her eyes gazing towards hope, towards help, and towards where Oliver waited for her.

Oliver then recalled details of testimony and forensic reports that his mother, Mary Bennett had been gagged with a handkerchief that was later recovered. This contained DNA evidence of both parties; from Mary, blood and mucus from having been so violently rammed into her mouth that it caused abrasions and had loosened teeth. But it also had DNA from the suspect Sullivan in the form of mucus, and was used to place him at the scene, and prove his involvement in the offence. The handkerchief was also heavily soiled, which indicated that it hit the ground either during the attempts to gag Mary or from where it had been later discarded.

Oliver also recalled from other images that one of his mother's earrings was found on the ground away from her body. Along the route taken from the lay-by. This suggested a struggle, or that she was dragged or carried.

It was determined that Mary died in the minutes after Sullivan had left her. It was apparent that she had made some efforts to move from where the attack had taken place back towards the road. These efforts were futile, and she only managed to move a couple of feet before succumbing to her injuries.

The Coroner's report stated that Mary Bennett died from repeated blows to the head, or *Blunt Force Trauma* as the report stated. Again, from the forensic examination of Sullivan upon his arrest, it was determined that this was most likely caused by his clenched fists. He was seen to have extensive bruising and a fractured metacarpal to his right hand when he was examined.

It was deemed to be a brutal rape, by a determined attacker. But when he was arrested mere hours after the assault he was found to have no attack marks on him. As a result, his defence centred around it being consensual between both parties. This was addressed in Court by a psychologist, who stated that it was likely that Mary didn't fight back in any way out of a sense of self-preservation for her, and for Oliver. She probably felt that if Sullivan took what he wanted from her then she would stand a better chance of escaping with her life, and of being able to protect her son.

Oliver crouched and wept. He now knelt on the exact spot where his mother had died, where she had not fought back or in any way tried to defend herself. She had allowed herself to be defiled, with the sole reason being to survive, to protect herself, and in turn to protect Oliver. Sullivan didn't need to kill her. He took what he wanted, her death was not essential to that. She could've been allowed to live, she didn't have to be taken from Oliver. For that, a debt must be settled.

It was starting to get dark when Oliver brought himself back from that moment to now. There was only one thing he still needed to do.

He stood up and went back through the opening, back into the lay-by, and to the van. He opened the back doors again. He put the saw back into a bag as he no longer had any need for it. He then took the last item he needed from one of the bags. It was a two-pack of vehicle towing ropes. He removed them from the packaging, which he discarded. Oliver also took the folding ladder, he ripped off the label and cut the ties which prevented it from falling open. He set the ladder down briefly in order to close the van doors.

Oliver then returned to the clearing with the items. He had already chosen which tree would be most suitable. The reason he chose to utilise a towing rope for his specific purpose was that it was the easiest and most convenient way of buying a length of rope with an eye, or metal ring and a clip, similar to a carabiner spliced into one end. This way Oliver could dispense with the need for a knot, and just feed the end of the rope through the eye in order to create a noose.

Oliver stood beneath his chosen tree. He then threw one end of the rope over a convenient bough. Once he caught the hanging end, he then attached the other end around a lower branch and clipped it back on itself. Then with the hanging end, he again clipped it back on itself to create the running loop. Oliver then tucked the hanging end out of sight. He hid the ladder under a bush and kicked some loose brush over it to avoid it being stolen or raising any suspicion. He hid the second rope with the ladder should it be needed. With everything in readiness, Oliver took one last look around, his last chance to see the clearing in daylight, before returning to the van. Then he cleared the back of the van of the shopping bags and the discarded packaging before heading off.

Chapter Twenty-Seven

That evening Oliver made the run from Sullivan's home to the lay-by once more. As before, he abided by all speed limits and traffic control. However, this time he intentionally took a slightly different route in the final stages of the journey. This was so he could approach the lay-by from the other direction and allow him to pull up with the lay-by on his nearside, and the sliding door to be nearest to the woodland. He used the marker of the dog waste bin to indicate exactly where he needed to park. From there, he alighted and walked round to the nearside of the van. He had parked perfectly, with the sliding side door immediately across from the gap in the foliage which he had earlier cleared and widened. There was one more thing to check.

Oliver opened the sliding side door. The only thing in the cargo area of the van was a tool bag, one that when unzipped the bag lay fully open, and everything contained therein was immediately accessible.

Oliver already had his head torch on, but he then took a unidirectional camping lantern from the bag. He then closed the door and locked the van before disappearing through the gap in the foliage.

He knew what the clearing looked like in daylight, he needed to know what it looked like in darkness. Once in the clearing, Oliver first went to the tree that he had earlier clipped the towing rope to. It was still there, just as he had left it. He then retrieved it from how he had concealed it and let it hang from the bough it had been thrown over. As it hung there, gently swinging in the last of its momentum, Oliver set the lantern on the ground with its beam towards the towing rope. He then took hold of it at the highest point he could reach. He lifted his feet from the ground and let the rope take his body weight. He could hear an occasional creak as the rope and tree settled into taking his weight. But after a few moments, there was silence. The only noises to be heard were the echoes of passing traffic from beyond the trees.

After he was sure that everything was in readiness, he sat down on the trunk of a felled tree, near to where the lantern had been left earlier, its beam cast on the towing rope. Oliver used the beam to look at his watch. It was still relatively early. He would have over an hour to wait in addition to driving back to Sullivan's if he left now.

He just sat there looking up at the rope, imagining that this would soon be a noose. Knowing that this was where his story would end. He looked back towards the opening, to the lay-by, towards the traffic, and the world beyond. He reminisced that it was an evening much like this one when his mother had stopped here. It was dark like it was now. When she was grabbed and dragged into this clearing, past where Oliver now sat, to where the crime scene photos had indicated her defiled body was later found. Where she had screamed for help but allowed herself to be raped, with the sole ambition of being allowed to live, so as to spare her son who was mere yards away.

Although the clearing was now in darkness, and in essence an unnerving place, Oliver felt strangely at ease. He knew what had happened, and what he was planning to do, but he felt at peace with both. To him, one justified the other, crime and punishment, cause and effect, action and reaction. What was about to happen had needed to be done all along, Oliver merely came up with the means. To him, he wasn't an avenging angel, he was just the vessel in which true justice was to be delivered.

Oliver checked his watch again, it was time to start heading back. He took a long slow inhalation as he stood. Firstly, he went back to the towing rope and concealed it behind the tree trunk as he had done before. He then retrieved his lantern and headed back towards the opening that led back to the lay-by.

Before he stepped through the opening, he turned and took one last look at the clearing. He wanted to appreciate one last moment of peace here, before unleashing carnage on this tranquillity. Lightning does indeed strike twice.

oOo

Oliver was able to drive back to Sullivan's any way he chose as this was not a timed run. He was able to fractionally break the speed limits and take discretion on traffic control. All that he had to do was *not* draw any attention to himself. As a result, he made the return trip ten minutes quicker than the outward journey from Sullivan's.

When Oliver arrived back at Sullivan's he parked in the area in front of the block. He was able to choose the last space on the left, the one closest to the side passage that led to the bins. It had been designated as a no parking area and was marked with yellow hatchings. This was to allow the refuse collectors to have easy access to the dumpsters without parked cars blocking their way. Oliver knew he wasn't going to be here for very long. He had seen cars parked there previously, so his being there wasn't going to cause any fuss, and there certainly wasn't going to be a bin collection in that time either. He had reversed into the bay so that the sliding side door would open onto the side passage, and not be impeded by any other parked cars.

Oliver alighted from the van. He was now wearing his army surplus poncho over the top of his normal clothes. He walked around the back of the block. As he cleared the corner he looked up, above him he could see lights on in Sullivan's flat. Everything was coming together, but for now, he must wait.

Chapter Twenty-Eight

As this was no longer a recce, a reconnaissance mission, gathering information about Sullivan, time was slowing as Oliver hid in the trees looking up at the flat.

The time for information gathering had passed, it was time to put his well-laid plan into effect. He had all the information he needed to know about Sullivan; who he was, his habits and routines, but most importantly, why they were both here on this night.

Oliver's whole life was about this one evening. Sullivan was the subliminal reason that had forged Oliver into the person he was to become. Sullivan was the reason that Oliver had developed the unhealthy fascination with medieval torture and capital punishment. He was the reason that Oliver had been over-zealous in school and in his karate classes. He was the reason Oliver had a righteous sense of right and wrong. He was also the reason behind all of the cognitive decisions that Oliver had made since joining the police. Oliver knew the processes behind complaints, he knew the likelihood of being put on restricted duties away from the front line if he had a complaint against him, and that this could ultimately lead to a suspension or eventually dismissal. At that point, he wouldn't care which. He just considered it convenient that he got his wish first time out when he roughed up Keenan. Had putting the hurt on Keenan not had the desired outcome, then efforts would have been made at every opportunity until such a complaint was eventually made.

Once on restricted duties, Oliver had the time and the freedom to investigate Sullivan in amongst the menial tasks he was to be allocated. The tasks never appeared to take long, and were soon out of the way, allowing Oliver ample time to complete *his* work. Had the suspension not come along as it did, Oliver also had a contingency of having some sickness planned. He didn't want to waste his annual leave, as getting that was troublesome enough according to Dave Cox, his mentor.

Everything in his life had been preparing him for this moment. He was set on a path, and the decisions ahead of him were no longer his to make. He no longer had any choice in his actions. What was to happen, had to happen.

As Oliver looked up at the window, he went through a list in his mind of all the items that he felt he needed at this moment in time. As he worked his way down the list he patted his pockets to verify that he had them, and their location on him. He wanted to be able to rely on muscle memory when he needed it the most, and not be rifling through pockets to find things when they were most urgently needed.

He was ready. He looked at his watch beneath the poncho to prevent the glow from the display being seen. He was now within the approximate time-frame that had been adopted all week. At any time from now on, the light in the presumed living room would go out and Sullivan would leave his flat. Oliver would be ready.

He didn't have to wait for much longer. The last remaining light in the top floor flat switched off, leaving the flat in darkness. Sullivan had left his flat.

Oliver had seconds to get into position. He began counting his mimicked time frame that would lead Sullivan out of the building. He was out of his poncho and running across the back garden to the corner of the building. There he would wait. He discarded the poncho on the ground at the corner of the building, it was right where he would need it later. The counting continued. He waited, any second now.

Chapter Twenty-Nine

Marc Sullivan reached for the TV remote and switched it off just as a soap-opera's opening sequence began to play. He chucked the remote down next to him where he sat on the sofa. He then picked up the can of cider that was on the table beside the sofa, he shook it and smiled approvingly that there was still some left in it. He swigged from the can, draining it in one mouthful, before setting it back down. He then stood with a groan.

The soap-opera indicated that it was time to take in his evening routine. One that was suggested to him by his GP, one designed to make him healthier, designed to get him some regular exercise in an attempt to lower his cholesterol, not to merely facilitate his cigarette habit.

Once standing, he reclaimed the cider can and walked across into the kitchenette, the only division between the kitchen and the living room was that the carpet changed to a linoleum floor covering. Sullivan placed the empty can next to a collection of others placed on the counter. There was no waste bin to put them in, and the carrier bag hung over the corner of a cupboard door to receive rubbish was in dire need of being changed.

Sullivan slipped his expensive white training shoes on. They were wasted in their only purpose as they had yet to see sporting activity of any kind. He then picked up and slipped on his jacket. He patted both side pockets to ensure his wallet and cigarettes were where he expected them to be.

He then scoured the kitchen counter surfaces for his keys and lighter. Seeing them both, he snatched them up and headed for the door. There was no hallway, the front door led from the kitchenette directly onto the communal landing. As he opened the front door, he switched off the lights. The lights Oliver saw go out.

One Mississippi.

Sullivan closed his front door behind him and locked it shut. He then started down the stairs

Four Mississippi.

Sullivan passed the first floor, he continued down.

Twelve Mississippi.

Sullivan reached the ground floor. He expected it to be cold outside, so he turned the collar of his jacket up. He stopped just inside the front door. He then reached into a pocket and he took out the packet of cigarettes, he opened it and took one out which he placed in his mouth ready to light once he was outside.

Twenty-One Mississippi.

Sullivan was now ready to face the cold. He took hold of the door handle, twisted it, pulled the door open. He felt the cold hit him in the face. He stepped outside.

Twenty-Seven Mississippi.

Sullivan stayed in the alcove, so he was out of the wind to light his cigarette. Once lit, he stepped out into the passageway. For a moment he looked to his left, towards the back of the block, before facing forwards again and turning towards the street.

As he took a couple of steps towards the street, it happened.

Chapter Thirty

As Marc Sullivan stepped out and away from his building he was struck firmly behind the left knee by something hard. The pain was instant and caused him to collapse to the ground as his leg could no longer hold his weight. As he landed, he rolled on to his back. In his view, silhouetted by the security light above the front door was a figure now standing menacingly over him. Before he could say or do anything other than experience and endure severe pain in his leg, he was hit in the face with a liquid spray. Initially, it felt as if he had been sprayed with a water pistol or super soaker, but then more pain followed. It became excruciating, it burned. His eyes started streaming. As the pain increased, so his vision decreased. His vision of this silhouetted figure became blurred, until nothing could be distinguished, all he could see were shades of darkness.

Sullivan lay there on the ground, writhing in agony, his hands rubbing feverishly at his eyes, trying to rub the pain from them. Then suddenly Sullivan found himself being rolled over, onto his front. He was in no fit state to protest or resist, he just wanted the pain to go away. He still had his hands on his face.

He felt a sudden pressing pain to his lower back, a crushing pain as if someone was kneeling on him; if those were his thoughts, he was right.

"Give me your hands," he heard an intentionally muffled and lowered voice say. Sullivan did nothing, he kept rubbing at his eyes, he wanted his hands for that if nothing else.

At the lack of response, Sullivan felt a sudden jolt in the pressure felt to his lower back, this caused him to yelp in pain.

"Give me your fucking hands," the voice repeated, only this time in a more venomous tone than before. Sullivan felt he had no option but to comply. He brought one hand down and away from his face and lowered it to his side. This hand was immediately grabbed and drawn behind his back. Sullivan then felt a tightness around his wrist, and the click-click of a metal-on-metal ratchet could be heard. He was being handcuffed.

"Give me your other hand," the voice then said. Sullivan was more reluctant to give his last hand up as he would no longer have anything to soothe the pain in his face. He then felt a sharp tug on the handcuffs which pulled at his wrist and elbow causing more pain than his face was enduring. So, he again complied. He then felt another sharp tug as this hand was brought around his back to meet the first. He was now cuffed with his hands behind his back. He momentarily struggled against the cuffs. He found the pain wasn't as bad as he'd experienced previously, because Oliver had closed the cuffs around his sleeves, instead of over bare skin.

"Are you the police?" Sullivan asked.

"Shut the fuck up, now stand up," the voice demanded of him.

His eyes burned, and his leg hurt, but he didn't want any more pain, so he complied, and with the assistance of his assailant he was able to stand. For a moment his leg refused to take his weight, and he relied on the wall for support before being able to stand unassisted.

Oliver could see that Sullivan needed a moment to compose himself and regain his balance on his injured leg. This he allowed him, but only for a moment, not a second longer. Oliver then

214

turned him to face the rear of the building. He took hold of the cuffs behind Sullivan and lifted them. This caused Sullivan to bend forward at the waist in a vain attempt to alleviate the pressure being imposed on his arms. Oliver then put further stress on Sullivan in this position by placing a hand at the back of his neck to keep his head as low as possible.

This position was a technique taught in the police as part of the 'cell placement' drill. It would in practice be performed by three officers, with one on each arm, and the third on the head. The reason for keeping the head low was to prevent the prisoner from being able to kick out or bite or spit at the officers. But, it also gives a sense of disorientation as they can only see their own feet, which psychologically gives a greater propensity to follow any instructions given.

Whilst in this stressed position Oliver was then able to lead Sullivan towards the back of the building. Once around the corner, Oliver retrieved his poncho from where he had earlier discarded it. He then draped it over Sullivan to further disorientate him.

About mid-way along the back of the building Sullivan started to struggle, maybe due to panic about being restrained, in pain and helplessly enveloped in a shroud. His efforts, however, were minimal due to his restraints, but Oliver dealt with this by slamming Sullivan against the wall, and telling him, "Fucking cut it out, okay!"

He then rounded the last corner, and Oliver could see the side of his van parked ahead. Nothing stood between them and the van now. They passed the area where the dumpsters were kept. The van loomed closer. Sullivan was putting up nothing further in the way of any protest.

Oliver stopped just prior to the corner of the building nearest his van, so he could reach into his pocket for the keys. He unlocked the van which was indicated by a flash of the hazard lights. He left Sullivan where he was for only a second or two, so he could approach the van on his own and slide open the side door. He then returned to Sullivan before he even had a chance to realise he no longer had hands on him.

The back of the van was now empty. Oliver had relocated the tool bag into the cab. There was nothing in the back of the van except for a roll of duct tape.

Oliver retrieved Sullivan and led him to the van. He then turned Sullivan so that he had his back turned to the open door. Oliver then pushed him backwards, so he sat on the floor of the van. Oliver then crouched down to lift his feet into the van and roll Sullivan onto his side. Oliver climbed into the back of the van himself and stepped one foot over Sullivan, straddling him.

Then using the duct tape, Oliver placed a strip across Sullivan's mouth, and also bound his feet together. Once this was complete and Oliver was sure that Sullivan was secure, he grabbed his poncho and jumped down from the back of the van and slammed shut the side door. He then walked around the back of the van to the driver's door. He climbed into the driver's seat. He took a moment to catch his breath and compose himself before starting the engine.

Then, after another deep breath, he selected first gear, released the handbrake, and slowly pulled out of the parking area onto Allingham Road to begin a now familiar journey.

Chapter Thirty-One

"Nine-nine-nine operator, which service do you require?" a voice said when the call was answered.

"Um, police, please," a panicked voice replied.

"Police, what's your emergency?" the call handler asked.

"Er, yes, hello, I think I've just seen someone being bundled into a van," the caller stated.

Over the next few minutes the call handler asked numerous questions, most of which the caller was able to answer. She stated that she was a resident in a hostel. That her flat was on the ground floor and overlooked the car park. She went on to say that she was in the process of closing her curtains for the evening when she saw what she thought was a man covered in a blanket being bundled into a white van before being driven off. She gave her address as Flat 2, 46 Allingham Road. She was also able to provide the full registration for the van, LV04KDU.

After the call was ended, this report was then reviewed and passed across to the Force Control room for deployment. The call handler then performed the necessary checks as a result of the call. This included a check to determine the owner of the vehicle as well as checks on the block of flats in which the caller lived, and, presumably, as did the person who was potentially in the back of the van.

The results of these checks were then added to the call log. This showed the current registered keeper of the van. It also showed the cross-referenced reports created as a result of the contact made by Oliver's Force requesting a welfare visit be conducted on Sullivan.

When this report was received by the Force Control room, it was decided to deploy one police unit to the location of the reported incident to determine who, if anyone was missing from the block and to establish more details from the caller. A second unit would be deployed to attend the home address of the registered keeper of the van to determine the vehicle's current whereabouts. Also, an alert would be raised on the Automatic Number Plate Recognition (ANPR) system, which would notify any readings should the van pass any ANPR cameras.

What Oliver already knew, and what the police would find out in time, is that the reason he bought the van so close to when he would need it was to evade the registered keeper check revealing anything. In this case, the record still showed the man who sold Oliver the van as being the keeper, so when the police visited him, all he'd be able to give was Sullivan's name and address as it was that information that Oliver gave when he bought the van from him. The only other information, which would in the short term be useless to the police, was a physical description of the buyer. Had the seller been expeditious, and the DVLA efficient in updating the keeper record, then the police would only be knocking on the same door they would be knocking at for Sullivan anyway.

Oliver had also taken the ANPR system into consideration and had paid close attention on the route the first time he had driven it in daylight, and he was confident that there were no ANPR cameras anywhere along the chosen route.

oOo

When the police unit attended the flat of the 999 caller, they weren't able to obtain any more information than what she was able to give over the phone. The caller again described what she had seen, her vantage point, and the route the van had taken when it had driven off. She wasn't able to give any details as to a description of either people involved; the person bundled into the van, or the person doing it, as she only saw them briefly, from a distance, and in relative darkness.

After leaving Flat 2, the attending police officer then called at all the other flats in the block. He was told to do his best to get a reply from Flat 15, Sullivan's flat, as a result of the previous attempts, and the warning given by Oliver's Force.

The officer was only able to get a response from about half of the flats in the block, no one was able to add anything relevant to the enquiry. As the officer had the foresight to call at Sullivan's flat first, and getting no reply, he was also able to ask the occupants of the other flats if they knew his whereabouts or had any contact details, including a mobile phone number for him. This was seen as a longshot given the premises, and the occupancy, but it was worth asking. No one had Sullivan's mobile number.

The only thing the officer was able to add of any relevance was that there was a whole cigarette and lighter discarded just outside of the front door. From here the officer scrutinised the outside perimeter of the building. When he fed this information back to the Force Control he was asked if a police dog unit would be required. This was ruled out, as it was determined all persons involved had left in a vehicle, and that the dog would only be able to track foot traffic.

The officer was told to remain at this location and to await further instructions. He was advised that an Intelligence Officer was doing some background checks on Sullivan regarding the enquiries made by Oliver's Force, with whom they were also liaising given this revelation.

Chapter Thirty-Two

The journey from Sullivan's home to the lay-by was uneventful. Oliver had become genuinely concerned for Sullivan about mid-way through the trip as he had gone quiet and had stopped wriggling around in the back of the van.

When he arrived in the lay-by, he found it was deserted. He parked in the exact same spot as he had done earlier that afternoon. As he pulled up, he gave himself a moment to calm himself, to take a breath before what was to come next. He compared this moment as possibly similar to that of a state-employed executioner on the morning of an execution. That calm moment where they wait outside the condemned cell before the appointed hour, and before being given the signal to proceed by the Governor or Sheriff. Much like the executioners of yesteryear, Oliver had undertaken meticulous preparations to ensure everything was ready for when it was required. But that's where the similarities ended. His studies into capital punishment methodology could only teach him the exact technicalities. The motives didn't lie with the executioners, it was down to the Courts of the day. The executioner was only a part of the process, a cog in the machine. In this case, Sullivan had already served the sentence as it was imposed by the Court of *his* day. But now he faced a different Justice.

Oliver waited for a gap in the traffic. No headlights ahead of him, none in the wing mirror. Now was his opportunity. He glanced behind him to check on Sullivan, he was still wriggling, though not as much as before. He was still alive.

Oliver got out of the cab. He walked around the front to the nearside of the van. As he walked around, he put his head torch back on. He stood between the van and the gap in the foliage. He looked through the gap, he couldn't see anything beyond the blackness. He listened, he couldn't hear anything beyond the soft hum of distant traffic. He took hold of the handle of the sliding door, he slid it open. This startled Sullivan who started squirming and struggling to get as far away from the noise that had startled him as possible.

This was the reason for buying the hi-top van. Oliver was able to get into the back of the van and stand up fully without any fear of banging his head on the roof. Once in there, he was able to subdue Sullivan.

"Quit fucking about, or I'll empty this whole fucking can in your face!" He directed the beam of his head torch at the can of police-issue CS spray that he held in his hand. Sullivan recognised the can, and he recognised the effects of it.

Then Sullivan squinted as the light from Oliver's head torch reflected off something metallic. A cutthroat razor that he had taken from his pocket. Sullivan tried to get away but found himself backed into a corner in the back of the van.

"I'm gonna cut your legs free," Oliver began, "if you kick out or do anything like that I'll end you right here. Do you understand?"

Sullivan tried to verbalise a response, remembering he couldn't due to the tape still across his mouth, he resigned himself to nodding enthusiastically without ever taking his eyes off the blade being held in front of him. Seeing him struggling to speak Oliver removed the tape from across his mouth.

"Do you understand?" Oliver repeated.

"Yes, yes," Sullivan hastily replied.

Having received the desired response, Oliver then cut across the tape that bound Sullivan's legs together. His reckless actions cut more than the tape as was evident in Sullivan wincing. It was further evident as when Sullivan parted his ankles that Oliver had cut through his jeans too, and that blood was seeping through from a concealed wound.

When Oliver had struck Sullivan behind the knee as he stepped out from the front door of his block of flats, he had used his police-issued extendable metal baton. He had sprayed him with his police-issued CS spray, and he cuffed him with his police-issued handcuffs. These were all items he had smuggled out during the times he was on restricted duties for just this occasion.

"You a cop?" Sullivan asked. Daring to ask a question, and willing to accept the consequences that came with the answer.

"I'm not a cop, not any more," came the reply, "you wanna know who I am? Well, I'll tell ya in a little bit."

Oliver then beckoned Sullivan to shuffle himself across the floor of the van on his backside until his legs were hanging out of the van.

Oliver then helped him to his feet and led him through the gap into the clearing.

Chapter Thirty-Three

The result of the Intelligence Officer's enquiries, as well as his liaising with his equal in Oliver's Force, hadn't turned up a great deal of information.

It was decided that all necessary steps must be taken to locate Sullivan as soon as possible, and potentially also PC Oliver Bennett.

Both Forces were now scrutinising the Mary Bennett case file to establish any details relevant to their current predicament. But as the report was closed, they were having to review it from page one of a paper file, as it was from electronic records inconsistent with their current computer systems.

They funnelled and filtered their review of the report, primarily focusing on persons and location involved. They were already trying to locate Sullivan by attending his current abode. The only other relevant party in the case was the victim, Mary Bennett. This, in turn, led to a request that a police officer again be sent to Bennett's home address to again try to determine the location of Oliver from his father.

The only other relevant location within the file was deemed to be where the actual attack took place. This location wasn't within the jurisdiction of either of the Forces currently involved. It was over the border into a third county. This would normally require making contact with this Force, and making the request for them to attend the location to determine if anything untoward was taking place there.

However, time was now deemed to be of the essence. The Intelligence Officer from Sullivan's local Force decided that a unit from his Force would be sent as a priority to the location where the original attack had taken place. This was in addition to making contact with the Force that covered that area requesting their urgent attendance.

Chapter Thirty-Four

Having walked Sullivan through the gap into the clearing Oliver pushed him, causing him to trip on the uneven ground and fall. Oliver dropped the tool bag he had brought from the van behind the same felled trunk he had earlier sat on

Oliver then sat on the trunk. He looked at the ground in front of where he had sat. The ground where his mother had breathed her last. He overlaid in his mind the images of her body onto the real world. Then he reverted his gaze back to Sullivan. He looked scared, and he looked pathetic.

"You asked me who I am?" Oliver said. The beam from his head torch striking Sullivan in the face, making it impossible for him to see any details of Oliver's face. This, however, was not his intention, as it was not necessary.

"You'll know who I am, we've met before, you and me," Oliver paused, "it was a long time ago, you probably don't remember. Near to where we are right now. You met my mother that night too. Ringing any bells yet?"

In an instant, the combination of the location and the circumstances being described began to add up for Sullivan. Oliver stood up and began pacing around where Sullivan lay on the ground. He found himself awkwardly trying to pivot around so as not to have his back turned towards Oliver. This was Oliver's intention.

"You grabbed her just out there," Oliver said as he cast the beam of his head torch back towards the gap that led to the lay-by. "I was only five years old when you took her from me."

Oliver then shone the beam back into Sullivan's face, he wanted to see his reaction, once he finally realised who his captor was. Sullivan did indeed now know who Oliver was. He also knew the gravity of the situation he was now faced with.

"You were *that* kid?" Sullivan asked.

As Oliver continued to circle around Sullivan, he said, "I *was* that kid. I stopped being a kid that very night because, not only did you steal the life from Mary Bennett, you stole my mother *and* you stole my childhood from me."

By this time, Oliver had circled around and had reached the tree with the towing rope thrown over a bough. He retrieved the rope from where he had concealed it behind the trunk and allowed the noose part of the rope to swing into the open. He directed the beam of his torch towards it, making it unmissable to Sullivan.

"Now, I'm here to pay what you're owed," Oliver said.

Realising his fate, a sudden look of terror came over Sullivan's face. He could not take his eyes off the noose that was still gently swinging before him.

"You can't, you can't do this," Sullivan began to plead, "I've done my time."

Oliver looked down at him, he had begun trembling uncontrollably. In a momentary loss of focus, Oliver's immaturity crept through. For the briefest of moments, all Oliver could think about was Dave's comment at seeing the nervous or cold Keenan in the back of the car. He too was *trembling like a shitting dog.* This caused Oliver to smile, a most inappropriate smile, and a smile that in the low light of the lantern looked nothing short of maniacal to the terrified Sullivan.

Oliver turned back towards Sullivan feeling he needed to compose himself, unaware of the increased terror his expression had caused.

"You've done your time, settled your debt, have you?" He laughed. "To society maybe, *not* to my family."

Oliver then walked back towards where Sullivan lay, but not in a circular motion as before, this time directly towards him, menacingly, and with purpose. He could see Sullivan squirming on the ground, trying to get purchase with his feet, but his once white and pristine, now filthy trainers kept slipping in the dirt. Oliver knelt down beside him, he tilted his head, so as to match the angle of Sullivan's.

"Do you *really* think you've paid the price for ending one life and destroying two others?" Oliver said. "You haven't even begun paying for it."

With that, Oliver stepped over Sullivan's prone body, deliberately catching him with a trailing foot. He walked over the felled trunk he had sat on and retrieved the tool bag from behind it. This was the first time Sullivan saw the bag.

"What the fuck is that?" he asked desperately.

"This?" Oliver said as he straddled Sullivan and lowered himself down, so that he was sitting across him. "This is so whoever finds you will know why this happened, coz neither of us is gonna be around to tell 'em."

Oliver then began rummaging through the tool bag looking for what he needed. As he rummaged, he began to explain to Sullivan what he was planning to do.

"Did you know, before it was abolished in 1789, that those convicted of murder, those like you, who somehow escaped the

228

death penalty were branded with a letter 'M' so everyone knew what they did. This was a one-time-only leniency, after that it was the rope. Ah, here it is…"

Oliver sat up from leaning over the bag, content he had found everything he needed. In his hand he held the same crème brûlée blow torch he had used before, as well as a pair of needle-nose pliers. He set them down at his side.

"They used to brand them with a letter, so everyone knew what offence they had committed; a 'T' for theft, 'F' for felon which covered pretty much everything else, basically just telling everyone you're a scumbag, and 'M' for a murderer, like *you*."

Oliver then reached under the collar of his jacket and pulled a pendant on a long silver coloured chain from inside his top. It was a pendant he had given his mother for her last birthday before she left him. The pendant was a metal 'M'. The 'M' was now blackened and didn't match the colour of the chain.

Sullivan saw the beam from the head torch glint off the metal 'M', he started to squirm beneath Oliver, sensing he knew what was coming next.

Feeling this beneath him, Oliver lifted his body weight slightly, before dropping it back down on Sullivan's abdomen. This winded him, and also caused pain by crushing his hands which were still cuffed behind him.

Oliver fumbled at his side to locate the pliers he had set down. He picked them up and brought them into Sullivan's view. Sullivan watched intently, with terrified fascination as Oliver placed the middle of the 'M' between the tips of the pliers. He then wrapped the chain around the handles and tucked it under his fingers. He then reached down again and retrieved the blowtorch.

Although it was fiddly, Oliver had practiced igniting it with one hand. The blue flame instantly drew Sullivan's attention. Oliver could feel him start to writhe beneath him again. The light from the flame outshone the light from the headtorch, and for the first time, Sullivan was able to see details of Oliver's face. He was just a kid, but he was a kid with a maniacal look on his face. They both stared at the flame, not a sound could be heard beyond the soft, almost soothing roar of the propane burner.

Then Oliver brought his hands closer together. The 'M' in the tips of the pliers was engulfed in the flame. This was the reason it was blackened and no longer matched the chain. Oliver had practiced this. He knew he would only get one chance at this, and he wanted to get it right.

The blue flame burned orange as the metal was introduced to the flame. It cast Oliver's shadow on the trees behind him. The flame danced brilliantly around the metal, and the metal glowed orange to embrace the flame. The moment had come.

Oliver snuffed the flame out on the blowtorch by cutting off the fuel. He set it down beside him again. As he did, the beam of the head torch was cast off to one side. Sullivan was now fixated on the glowing metal in front of him, knowing exactly what was going to come next.

Oliver then leaned forward, he rested his elbow on Sullivan's chest. He then used his free hand to turn Sullivan's head to one side, so that his left cheek was uppermost. Fear could be seen as the glowing metal descended closer to him. He could see its brilliance, he could now feel its warmth. He started to writhe again.

Oliver joked. "Lay still, I don't want you getting this in your eye."

Sullivan closed his eyes as the metal descended further.

Screams could be heard echoing throughout the clearing as Oliver pressed the glowing metal against Sullivan's left cheek. Smoke rose from his face, and the distinct smell of burning flesh filled their nostrils.

After only a second, Oliver removed the now blackened and cooling metal from Sullivan's face. He cast the beam of his head torch on the cheek and admired his handiwork. Satisfied at a job well done. He set the pliers and their charred contents down next to the blow torch. He then looked back at Sullivan. He was writhing in agony beneath him. This was nothing compared to the pain he had caused his mother that night. His blood deserved to be spilled here.

As the pain in his face started to subside, Sullivan developed a new defiance. Adrenaline now coursed through his veins which had given him new confidence and impetus to challenge his fate.

"I think you've overlooked a couple of small things, boy," he said defiantly to Oliver.

"Oh yeah, and what are those?" Oliver replied.

"For someone who claims to know so much about this stuff, you ain't got a clue how to hang someone."

Oliver looked over at the noose, to where it was gently swinging in the breeze.

"Go on," he said.

"Ain't high enough off the ground to do any damage, besides, how you gonna get my head through that noose? Coz I sure as fuck ain't gonna make it easy for ya!"

A sly smile came over Oliver's face; by now this was wasted on Sullivan as his face was again engulfed in darkness.

"Well, you see, I've thought of that already you fat fucker," Oliver said as he stood up. "Back in a mo..."

With that he disappeared out of sight behind the tree again for a moment. Though not long enough for Sullivan to even give consideration to struggling against his bonds, or even attempting to get up. Besides that, Oliver had his curiosity, and anger given the insult despite his predicament.

Oliver returned into view carrying the four-way ladder. It was still folded up, just as he had left it. All Oliver had done since purchasing it was to remove the packaging and ties. He placed it on the ground next to Sullivan, and proceeded to unfold it from its concertina-like state.

"Y'see, I've already thought of that, and planned ahead. Now what I plan to do is this..." Oliver said as he finished unfolding it into a single straight ladder. He then stood up in order to be able to gesticulate to illustrate his commentary.

"I'm gonna strap you to this ladder using these," Oliver said as he pulled some heavy-duty cable ties from his pocket.

"Then I'm gonna prop you up against the tree. Once you're up there, I can then put the noose around your neck, easy-peasy. And then I can collapse the bottom of the ladder and watch you hang. Now, tell me, does that answer your question?"

Sullivan looked on with horror. The attention to preparation and contingency Oliver had paid was chilling. "Then, once you're hanging," Oliver continued. "I'll cut the ties and take the ladder away, then I'll take the handcuffs off, and leave you there. I mean there was a reason I cuffed you *over* your coat sleeves, and it *wasn't* me being kind. I didn't want you injuring yourself if you struggled too much. Who knows, they may even rule it a suicide? Y'know, one of those *couldn't live with the guilt and shame of it*, type situations, I mean, why else would you did come back to the scene of the crime... But, even if they don't, I really don't give a shit!"

In order for Oliver to fix Sullivan to the ladder he had to thread his cuffed arms through the ladder between two rungs, and in order to accomplish this Oliver needed Sullivan to be on his front, or at the very least, his side.

As Sullivan had already eluded, he was not planning on assisting Oliver in any way, and this was no exception.

The time for talking was explanation and rationality was over. It was time for Oliver to make good on all the promises he had made to himself. He stood up and approached where Sullivan lay before him.

Again, Oliver had given this aspect as much thought as everything else. He knew he could be vulnerable if he tried to roll Sullivan over from one side, but he deemed he was less vulnerable if he straddled Sullivan and kept low enough for any flailing legs to be ineffective. Sullivan anticipated Oliver's action, and as Oliver stepped over him he saw an opportunity, and he wasn't going to waste it. In an instant, Sullivan used his legs to bring himself to a semi-seated position. This, in turn, had the effect of knocking Oliver off balance, causing his left leg to come rising towards Sullivan's face. Sullivan thrust his head forward and buried his teeth into what he could reach of Oliver's thigh. He bit hard, he knew this was his only chance, and he wasn't going to waste it. He could feel his teeth sinking ever deeper. He could taste blood. He wasn't sure if it was Oliver's or his own. Then the leg was taken from him.

Now it was Oliver's turn to writhe in pain. He fell off to Sullivan's left side. Oliver clutched at his leg. Blood was coming through between his fingers. He cried out in pain though there was no one there who cared to listen.

Sullivan had rolled onto his side, from there he was able to get himself to his feet. He turned a quick three-sixty to determine the best direction in which to escape. The only light apart from Oliver's head torch was the occasional vehicle on the road beyond the trees. He looked down at Oliver on the ground, still clutching his thigh. Sullivan viciously kicked out at the light beneath him, knowing that if he was on target he would be kicking the boy in the head. A single well-placed kick reduced them to darkness. Sullivan was on his feet, and he ran towards the only remaining light.

He had a head-start on Oliver, and he was going to take full advantage of it. The ground was undulating and covered with debris. This caused Sullivan to lose his footing a couple of times, but the safety of the lay-by and the road beyond it was getting closer.

He stumbled as he came down the bank that separated the clearing from the treeline.

Sullivan kept running. He could now hear footsteps and yelling coming from behind him. Footsteps that would bring his captor with them, and surely also bring a one-way ticket back to the noose and promises of more pain.

The footsteps were closing in behind him. Getting louder, faster. His captor was injured, but this didn't seem to be impeding him. In a panic, Sullivan looked behind him to see how close his captor actually was, but all he could now see was blackness. He wasn't going to have a chance to let his vision accustom to the dark. He didn't know how far he had run from him.

Sullivan passed through the gap in the foliage and immediately slammed into the side of the Transit van. He realised this would tell his captor exactly where he was. He had a choice now, left or right. Sullivan had impacted the van on his right side, he now faced the front of the van. He ran to the left, towards the front of the van. He caught the wing mirror with his shoulder as he ran past it ripping it from its mounting.

Once clear of the van, Sullivan continued to run along the length of the lay-by. Unknown to him, a car approached from behind and passed him without him noticing it until it was all too late to get the attention of the driver. He yelled at the car as it began to disappear into the distance. Then from beyond the car, coming towards him, he could see the headlights of another vehicle. With the single focus of salvation in his mind, Sullivan ran into the carriageway, so he was more prominent for his oncoming saviour to see him. This vehicle *had* to see him.

Sullivan now stood in the road. He couldn't wave or do anything to attract the driver's attention any further as he was still handcuffed. All he could do was make himself as prominent as possible. As the vehicle approached, he shouted for help. Sullivan could make out that this was a people carrier, or MPV. He could see the front of the vehicle suddenly dip as the brakes were being applied. The driver had seen him, it was slowing down, and he was to be saved.

For the briefest moment, Sullivan breathed a sigh of relief in amongst his efforts to catch his breath. This was then followed by an all too late warning horn, coming from behind him. Sullivan turned. He finally had empathy for a deer in headlights, as he froze. The horn ceased, only to be replaced with the sickening high pitched screech of tyres on asphalt. Sullivan had just enough time to register that the screech was coming from an articulated lorry that was thundering down on him.

oOo

Oliver struggled to get to his feet. As his legs took his body weight he began to feel the pain of the injuries Sullivan had inflicted upon him coursing through his body. The pain made him delirious. For a moment he was struggling to make sense of what had just happened. In an instant, he had gone from having complete control of the situation, to now not knowing what was going on, and more importantly, where Sullivan was.

Oliver didn't see in which direction Sullivan had fled. From where Oliver now stood, he could've have gone in any direction in a one-hundred-and-eighty-degree arc, or back through the hedge towards the road. Oliver deduced this as being the most likely, as anything else would require him to negotiate undulating ground in total darkness, whilst handcuffed. Had he gone anywhere else, he would be greatly hindered.

Oliver had become momentarily disorientated, and it took a moment for him to realise the direction of the road beyond the hedge line. Only once a vehicle passed, was he sure which direction he needed to move in. He trained the beam of his torch on the opening in the hedge, and once aligned with it the beam reflected off the white paint of his van. He ran towards it and slammed into the side of the van much as Sullivan had done.

As with Sullivan, Oliver had to choose, to go towards the front, or to the rear. Again, as Sullivan had, Oliver had let instinct make the choice for him. He had impacted the van on his left side, so he faced towards the rear, and it was in this direction he ran. As he ran towards the rear of the van he heard the bullhorn of a lorry sound.

Oliver reached the rear of the van as the horn ceased, however, this was only to be replaced by screeching tyres. Oliver emerged from the back of the van. He looked ahead of the lorry passing him in time to see Sullivan standing in the carriageway ahead of it.

At the sound of the horn, Sullivan had turned to face towards the lorry, and also towards Oliver. For a moment, as the lorry went thundering past where Oliver stood, and as Sullivan was caught in the lorry's headlights, their gazes met.

Then Sullivan disappeared from Oliver's view as the lorry struck him. It was Oliver's turn to freeze as the lorry passed beyond where Sullivan had stood. A twisted and contorted body emerged from the rear of the lorry, illuminated only by the brakes lights of the lorry as it slowed to a halt. The MPV that had been Sullivan's reason for being in the road had also passed by and had stopped further down in the other direction having seen what had happened.

Oliver surveyed the pathetic heap as it came to rest in the carriageway. He then moved towards it, walking at first, before breaking into a run. When he reached the body, he straddled it and grabbed hold of Sullivan's jacket lapels, he then hoisted his torso from the road surface. Sullivan's head fell backwards. Oliver dropped him, and then knelt down over him. Engulfed in rage, he began flailing punches at the handcuffed and motionless body beneath him.

In the distance sirens could still be heard, only this time they had direction, they were getting closer. Also, blue lights flashed off the top of the trees like lightning. Oliver was oblivious to this, he was single-mindedly focused on pounding every last ounce of life out of Sullivan.

Blue lights approached, and sirens wailed, they echoed along the tree-lined passage towards where Oliver knelt over Sullivan. Almost simultaneously, police vehicles arrived on both sides, they stopped beyond where the lorry and MPV had parked.

The sirens ceased. The only noise to break the silence was the wails and cries from Oliver as he still continued to punch the body beneath him.

Running footsteps approached him as police officers ran past where the lorry driver and occupants of the MPV had got out to see what was happening in the road. Oliver was oblivious, still he straddled Sullivan, and still he punched. Voices cried out to him to cease, he didn't hear them.

Oliver then felt himself being dragged away. He couldn't feel any hands on him, he couldn't feel his own hands. He had no strength to resist them, he had nothing left. All his fight had been used up.

Oliver was restrained in the carriageway. He was forced to the ground and handcuffed. He did nothing to resist, although he couldn't comply with any instructions given, as he simply couldn't hear anything being said to him. He was catatonic. Once secured, he was brought to his feet and led towards the nearest police car, near to the MPV, and sat in the backseat.

As further police units attended, the road was closed. Eventually, an ambulance attended and was allowed through the closures to attend the scene.

Eventually, a more senior officer, the Duty Inspector, attended the scene. As he approached on foot he surveyed the carnage. From where he stood he could see a man under police guard in the back of a police car, and beyond him he could also see Paramedics tending to a prone body in the road.

He approached where Oliver was handcuffed in the back of a police car.

"Has he been nicked?" he asked one of the police officers watching over Oliver.

When he got the response he was expecting from his officer, he replied in an authoritative voice, "Get him out of here then, he doesn't need to be here any more."

The first officer acknowledged his colleague. He then shut Oliver's door and they both went around to get in the other side of the car. As they did so the Inspector followed them around. He leaned on the roof of the car, suggesting to the driver that he wanted to say something to him. The driver then dropped his window.

"Yes, sir?" The officer enquired.

The Inspector then continued, "But take good care of him, he's one of ours."

Epilogue

Oliver was arrested having been detained in the road after Sullivan was struck and killed by the articulated lorry.

The cause of death was concluded to be as a result of the road traffic collision. As a result, Oliver was initially only charged with kidnapping and assault occasioning grievous bodily harm of Sullivan. This was later added to numerous offences relating to unauthorised use of police databases and stealing police equipment.

The complaint filed by Ryan Keenan was upheld, and on the basis of that and the other charges, Oliver Bennett was dismissed from his role as a police officer with immediate effect.

At his trial, the list of charges took several minutes to read out in its entirety. The charges eventually included conspiracy to commit murder and the kidnapping of Marc Sullivan, as well as several counts of grievous bodily harm, including that of Ryan Keenan. It also included theft of police property, which referred to his handcuffs, baton and incapacitant spray, as well as breaches of data protection, and unauthorised use of police databases.

Oliver entered a guilty plea to all charges, which saw his father break down in tears in the public gallery. Following his plea, a statement was read before the court, penned by his counsel, designed to mitigate the sentence imposed for such crimes. Oliver is currently awaiting his sentencing hearing.

Finally, following Oliver's intervention, the night that left the individual stricken in the driveway, the perpetrator was arrested, charged and convicted of causing unnecessary suffering to wild and domesticated animals.

Lastly, Nimbus, the cat which was in the process of being attacked when Oliver intervened, survived his ordeal that night unscathed and is still alive to this day.